More Praise for *Watched*

"In this beautiful and intelligent novel, Marina Budhos explores whether the ties of family, community, and faith can save an immigrant Muslim teenager. No one who reads it will come away without empathy and compassion for the thousands of Naeems in this nation."
—Patricia McCormick, author of *Sold*

"*Watched* will pull you into its world with magnetic, graceful power and deeply touching scenes of immigrant life and relationships. A hauntingly perfect, potent story for this moment."
—Naomi Shihab Nye, author of *Habibi*

"I loved this book, a tense, realistic thriller set right now in a time of homeland insecurity."
—Robert Lipsyte, author of *The Contender*

"Riveting. Naeem is a wonderful character, full of heart, conflicted, lost in his own gorgeously, grittily depicted multicultural neighborhood."
—Tanuja Desai Hidier, author of *Born Confused*

"Naeem's experiences mirror . . . those of many Muslim, Arab, and South Asian teenagers navigating post-9/11 America."
—Deepa Iyer, author of *We Too Sing America*

"Delving into the real human costs of today's surveillance culture, *Watched* reveals profound immigrant truths about survival and betrayal, and what it really means to feel like you belong. Everyone should read this necessary book."
—Moustafa Bayoumi, author of *This Muslim American Life* and *How Does It Feel to be a Problem?*

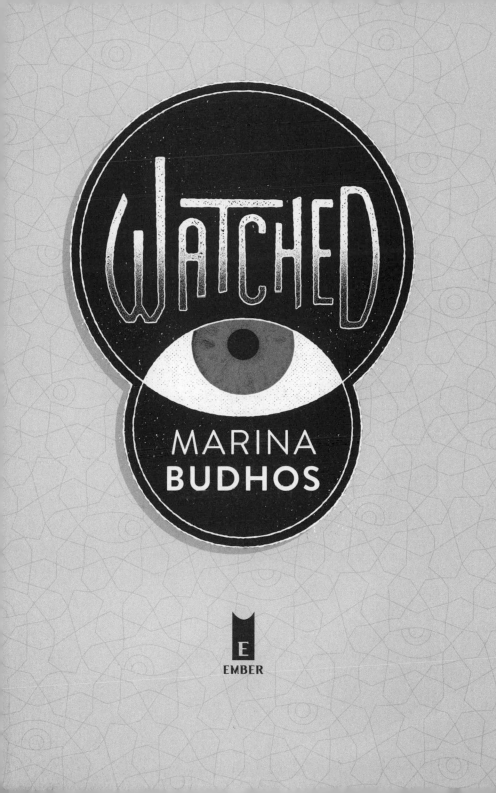

WATCHED

MARINA
BUDHOS

EMBER

All rights reserved. Published in the United States by Ember, an imprint of Random House Children's Books, a division of Penguin Random House LLC, New York. Originally published in hardcover in the United States by Wendy Lamb Books, an imprint of Random House Children's Books, New York, in 2016.

Ember and the E colophon are registered trademarks of Penguin Random House LLC.

Visit us on the Web! GetUnderlined.com
Educators and librarians, for a variety of teaching tools,
visit us at RHTeachersLibrarians.com

The Library of Congress has cataloged the hardcover edition of this work as follows:
Names: Budhos, Marina Tamar, author.
Title: Watched / Marina Budhos.
Description: New York : Wendy Lamb Books, [2016] | Summary: Far from the "model teen," Naeem moves fast to outrun the eyes of his hardworking Bangladeshi parents, their gossipy neighbors, and the other forms of surveillance in his immigrant neighborhood in Queens, but when his mistakes catch up with him and the police offer a dark deal, will Naeem be a hero or a traitor?
Identifiers: LCCN 2015046828 (print) | LCCN 2016037169 (ebook) |
ISBN 978-0-553-53418-4 (hardback) | ISBN 978-0-553-53419-1 (lib. bdg.) |
ISBN 978-0-553-53421-4 (pbk.) | ISBN 978-0-553-53420-7 (ebook)
Subjects: LCSH: Bangladeshi Americans—Juvenile fiction. | CYAC: Bangladeshi Americans—Fiction. | Muslims—Fiction. | Surveillance—Fiction. | New York (N.Y.)—Fiction. | BISAC: JUVENILE FICTION / People & Places / United States / Other. | JUVENILE FICTION / Social Issues / Adolescence.
Classification: LCC PZ7.B8827 Wat 2016 (print) | LCC PZ7.B8827 (ebook) |
DDC [Fic]—dc23

Printed in the United States of America

10 9 8 7 6 5 4 3 2 1

First Ember Edition 2018

To Sasha & Rafi
Heroes & Brothers

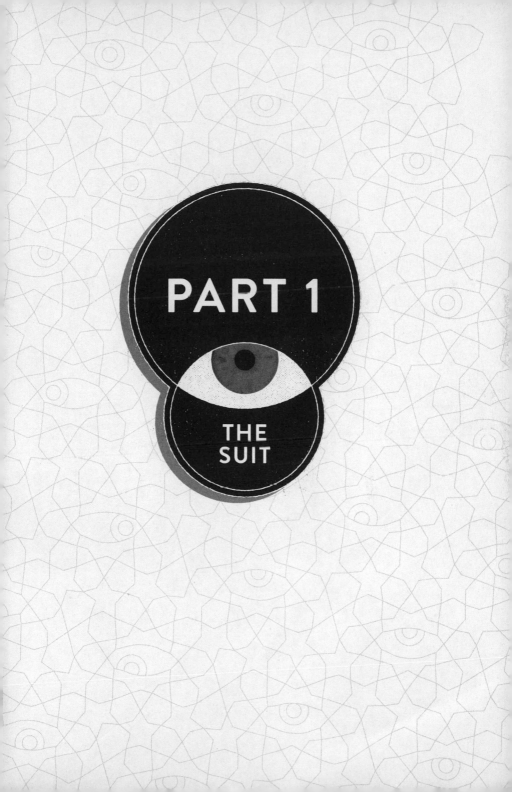

PART 1

THE
SUIT

FILE

Subject: Rashid Ahmed, Owner, Star Travel Agency
Address: XXXX 35th Avenue, Suite 211, Jackson Heights, NY
              11372
DOB: XXXXXXXX
SSN: XXXXXXXXX
Mosque: Al-Noor Masjid

- OP #293 spoke to Abdhul Rahman, lessee of store below Star Travel Agency. Rahman's country of origin is Bangladesh. Appeared nervous when asked about neighbor upstairs. Confirmed after-hours activity. Claims little affiliation. He is aware that the travel agency accepts cash for tickets and he does sometimes hold payments and packages in his store when the agency is closed.

Plan of Action

- Reinterview downstairs tenant.
- Continue mail cover.
- Ascertain whether use of cash is common for tickets bought to South Asia and other overseas destinations.
- Subpoena phone records and submit for analysis.
- Continue surveillance.

CHAPTER 1

I'M WATCHED.

There's a streetlight near my parents' store, and I hear the click, a shutter snapping as I round the corner. My gaze swivels up, but there's nothing. Just a white-eyed orb, a lamp, ticking. The dim sky floating behind. I shiver, tell myself it's all in my head. Nothing.

Click. Click.

Hunching my shoulders, I hurry down Thirty-Seventh Avenue, the sweat warm against my sweatshirt hood—past the thin shed of a shop with glittery bangles and cheap plastic frogs swimming in plastic tubs, past Mr. Rahman's table of beads hung on metal hooks, folded prayer rugs and little engraved Qurans. He, along with the other uncles who stand on the street, scans me, disapproving. They know. I'm up to no good. I'm not working in my parents' little store, as I should be.

I did spend most of the afternoon there, my stepmother hovering by the cash register, pretending to tally the day's earnings, but really she was grazing me like a worried searchlight. Her pencil tapping the side of the register. I know that look. *I see you.*

simile

Usually when it isn't busy in the store, and I've finished tying up the old newspapers and moving around the milk cartons, I sit on a crate in the back, next to the humming refrigerator, textbook balanced on my knees. But today it was hard to focus. My brain danced; I got antsy, thinking of where I'd rather be.

personification

The store was quiet. Only one customer—a *desi* guy, tweed jacket, jeans, blowing on his Starbucks coffee. He comes in a lot. "You have Post-its?" he asked. My stepmother shook her head. Disappointed, he bought some Tic Tacs.

Then my phone vibrated against my thigh. I always keep it on silent when I'm in my parents' store. *Meet me at the mall 4:30,* Ibrahim texted. *Urgent!* It's always urgent with Ibrahim.

Slamming the book shut, I jerked up from the crate. My concentration was shot. Whenever I hear from Ibrahim it's like a bowling ball cracking into the pins in my head, all my thoughts toppling over. There's no hope of picking my way through pre-cal equations.

simile

"Hey, Ma." I said this shyly, the way it always is between us. "I gotta go. Anything more you need?"

She glanced at me, alarmed. The eraser on her pencil did a little bob. "What about studying?"

"That's what I'm going to do," I lied. "Meet a friend. We've got pre-cal finals coming up."

Here her expression went sad, wistful. "Calculus, yes," she sighed. "When I was in high school I am getting eighty-five in this subject."

I feel bad for Amma. I call her Amma, as if she is my own mother, not my stepmom. She's always speaking English with me, not Bangla, trying to show how she was almost like an American-born, going all the way through twelfth grade, until her parents arranged a marriage to my father.

I knew Amma just wanted me to keep her company. But I couldn't help myself. I needed to get out of that little gloomy corner, everything so dusty and sad. Even the lottery ticket flyer—the only reason folks come in here—is peeling off the wall. The boxes of sugar cubes that have sat on the shelf since the store opened up. *Abba, who buys sugar cubes?* I want to shout. He's lost track of what they're doing with this place. It kills me, seeing all the customers hurry into the store across the street, the one that has the fresh new awning and fancy lettering, plastic chairs outside, and is always changing its stock, offering discounts. Or their friends, who have gotten together and opened a food mart with huge fish tanks and a halal butcher. *They have capital*, my stepmother sighs. *We have nothing.*

"Wait, I am showing you my outfit?"

I shot her a puzzled look.

"For graduation!"

I shook my head. "Ma, it's six weeks away!"

"No matter. Shop is having sale."

She bustled to the back of the store, where she'd hung a shalwar kameez on a hook on the back of the door, then brought it to the front, spreading the rustling plastic across the counter. "See!" she said proudly. "I even have it dry cleaned, so it is all ready."

This made me sad and angry too. Amma saved every bit of extra money—fifty cents here, a dollar from the groceries, stowing it in her empty tin of Darjeeling tea leaves. The outfit was beautiful—sea green, with blue beads dangling from the yoke like ice drops. But half the reason she was making such a big deal over this was because of me, and half because of her, all she gave up to marry my father.

"That's really nice, Ma."

"And your father, he is inviting many people to celebrate."

We both looked through the window, where we could see my father standing just outside the store, under the awning. His hands were tucked at the small of his back, his stomach pushed forward. More and more that's all he does: opens the store, puts away the Snapple bottles and milk cartons, and then leaves the rest to Amma. He sighs. He walks the pavement. Chats with the other shopkeepers. Complains about his bad knee. Mostly, he stares off at the rooftops, as if trying to glimpse something, just beyond, that escapes him.

Simile

The watching, it seeps into everything in our neighborhood. It's like weather, the barometric pressure lowering. Before the monsoons came in Bangladesh, you could feel the air thicken and squat on your head. A constant ache behind your eyeballs.   *personification*

For the past few years there's been another kind of pressure: a vibration around us, the air pressing down, muffling our mouths. We see the men, coming down the metal stairs from the elevated subway, or parked in cars for hours on end: clean-cut guys, creased khakis, rolled-up sleeves. The breath of Manhattan steaming off their clothes. They aren't from around here—that we can tell. Not like the young couples with their big padded strollers. Or the girls with peacoats and holes in their black tights, who moved to the nice part of Jackson Heights, carry yoga mats in cloth bags from stores I've never heard of. No, these people are different. They stroll into stores, finger the edges of the newspapers in their racks, check out flyers taped to the side of the fridge.

One day two of them came into my parents' store, pretended to buy some gum, and then asked a few questions about the travel agency upstairs. *Where is the man who runs the place? Mr. Ahmed? How often does he come in? Does he stay after hours?*

Abba shook his head. "I do not watch my neighbor so much. He is from Pakistan, that is all I know."

"Yet you hold packages for him?"

"Yes, but that is because they are not open all the time. It is favor."

The man consulted a tiny notebook. "You attend the same mosque? Al-Noor Masjid?"

At this, Abba froze, fingers resting light on the register, staring at the door. "No, we are praying at different place." It hurt my heart, hearing this. Abba's English, when he spoke to strangers, was halting, yet proper. He'd studied some English in Bangladesh and hated sounding uneducated to Americans.

Oxymoron

"Abba?" I whispered after the detectives left, and touched his arm. "You okay?"

He stirred and blinked. "I am fine." But his voice was rough at the edges. *metaphor*

It's his accepting, his hemmed-in air, his giving up that makes me crazy. The way he makes that sad gargling noise at the back of his throat, just stands here, rocking on his shoes. Or shuffles to the back of the store to pray. Lets those men scare him. *It's in Allah's hands. Nothing more to do,* he says.

Fight them! I want to cry. *Fight me!*

But he doesn't. He's too tired. Tired of his own years, first doing construction in Dubai, then in Brooklyn, long days up on the scaffolding scraping cement, a new wife and son, now the store, where every month he and my stepmother lean their heads together, write the rent check. *One more month,* he sighs. *Then maybe we close up.*

"I gotta go, Abba," I said, standing beside him now. I pointed to my backpack, as if to prove myself.

He just turned his face away.

Now I'm moving fast, just as I like it, wind cooling the sweat around my neck. I turn the corner, heading into the thick of the neighborhood—Seventy-Fourth Street—where the big grocery stores and sari shops with decked-out models and jewelry places draped in shiny gold are. I avoid the old men who know me, the ones sitting on crates, handing out laminated ads for astrology readings, phone cards. This is what I like, what I need. To move, always.

Once more the phone vibrates against my hip bone. *Are you coming?*

Annoyed, I text back. *Yes!*

Ibrahim forgets. He forgets I'm still in school. He's not. Or he is and he isn't. He's two years older than me and he's supposed to be at LaGuardia Community College, studying business. But who knows what he's actually doing. He's always got plans. A wireless store with his cousins. Maybe a restaurant.

It's not like Ibrahim and I are really friends. We're not. More on and off.

He texts me out of the blue, drives up outside the high school in a gleaming car, leans forward in his aviator shades and grins, and we spin off to a diner or taxi haunts. Maybe a movie, sitting deep in the bucket seats, gorging on a jumbo popcorn. Man, does that feel good. How many high school seniors get a pickup like that?

Just as I'm passing Mr. Khan's market, there, in the bins, next to the green and orange mangoes, the spindly okra, is a mound of glistening purple-blue plums. I can't help myself. My fingers shoot out, swipe one into my palm. Just a stupid little thing, easy to steal, now stowed in my sweatshirt pocket. Mr. Khan would give it to me if I asked. But that's no fun.

Before I can back away, a smiling Mrs. Khan is pushing through the doorway, strips of thick plastic bouncing against her broad shoulders. "How is your father?" she asks.

"Okay." I step back, anxious. The plum is nestled in my pocket, against my belly. Weirdly, I like the sweat pricking the back of my neck, the corkscrew of fear in my stomach.

"Business not so good, hah?"

"No. Not really."

"And where are you going?"

I point to my backpack. "Studying with a friend."

"Such a handsome boy!" she says, smiling, which makes my cheeks go hot. "Your parents, they are so proud of you. I am hearing you are in some kind of play?"

My heart gives a little pinch. *Proud.* I wish that were so. "Yeah," I tell her. "I was in *Grease.* At the high school."

"Very nice, very nice." She squints. "But this is not job. You are studying what?"

I stare down at my feet, frustrated. How many times have I had this conversation? With Abba, with the uncles and aunties who all want us to major in accounting or be doctors. That's just not in the cards for me. That much I know.

"It's just for fun, Auntie," I say.

She turns stern, leaning in. "But I see you one day with that girl? The Spanish one who washes hair at salon?"

"No, Auntie," I groan. "That was just a goof. I walked her home, that's all."

"Be careful," she warns. "These girls, they are always wanting to get boys like you with such nice hair. They think you make nice husband. You should stay and help your parents. When it is time for girl, they will find."

She smiles in a crinkly way that seems like a frown too. A lot of the elders in this neighborhood are like that—their joy is always laced with worry.

"Go on," she tells me. "You have work to do."

Relieved, I hurry away, only to see a cop strolling down the street right toward me. My bones seize up. The plum bumps chilled in my pocket. He looks like a nice guy—a little pudgy, thumbs loose on his belt, enjoying the sari shops, the old aunties pulling their cloth-covered carts, expertly pressing eggplants, checking for bruises. I remember what my stepmother always says: *You see a policeman, you never run, you understand, beta? They are not like policemen in Bangladesh, always asking for bribe. But still you smile at them nicely.*

Click-click.

The cop passes me, not even a glance. It's weird, this watching. You sense your own body, all its flaws, blown up, as if pixelated on a screen. I can see my neck, which is geeky-long, the soft flaps of my ears, which stick out as if I'm still four. I'm lit up, noticed in ways I don't want. This happens all the time.

Over at the playground park, the cops park their squad cars at an angle, eating their lunches inside. I can see their eyes, hidden in the cool cave of their cars, on me and my friends. Or sometimes when I'm late for school, I'll see some kid not much older than me, with his hands splayed on the greasy subway tile, cops giving him a pat-down. I feel dirty on his behalf. I just want to wash myself clean.

Two blocks away, the elevated track rises, throwing its shafts of broken shadow. I can hear the shuttle and clack of a train sliding into the station. I'm sure Ibrahim is at the entrance to the mall, tapping his sneaker, furious.

At the turnstiles, I see another cop, whose eyes bore straight through me, see the plum, radiate it, *poof*, in super-hero smoke. Fingers shaking, I start to slide my MetroCard.

"Hey."

I freeze.

"Let me see."

He saunters over, glances at my card with the student seal, gives me the once-over. I wish I had a chance to hitch up my jeans so the band of my underwear doesn't show. But I can't. Reaching for my waist—he might take it the wrong way.

"You a student?"

"Yes, sir. Newtown High, sir."

"Your age?"

14

"Eighteen."

He nods.

My right knee is jiggling something bad.

"Okay. Go ahead."

Then I'm dashing up the platform, fast, sneakers blurred. It's only when the train slides out of the station that my heart stops thumping like a bass and my cell phone vibrates in my pocket, against my thigh. *simile*

Where are u???

Coming, I tap back.

I bring out the plum. It's still sweaty cold. I touch it to my mouth, break the skin. It's sweet.

CHAPTER 2

THERE WAS A BEFORE.

When I didn't do stupid dares, didn't lie to my parents, and didn't snatch plums from neighborhood friends.

When I was a gift, a firstborn. "Sweet Naeem. Butter boy, knees so fat we can count his dimples!" My mother, bless her soul, used to say this about me. We lived with Abba at home, back in Dhaka, Bangladesh, then, and he would draw back the mosquito netting and hoist me up near the window to admire everything about me: my plump fingers, my chortle-laugh, my blue-black curls. He kept a photo of me tacked to his locker when he lived on the construction site in the Gulf, and carried it with him when he came to Brooklyn and learned how to mix cement for the fancy brownstones in Park Slope, Bed-Stuy.

In Dhaka, we lived in an apartment on the sixth floor,

looking out on a rubbled lot where they were supposed to build more. In those days, just around the time Amma needed to pull the curtains shut from the midday glare, he arrived for his rice and vegetables, which my mother would set out on the plastic tablecloth. I would play at their feet while they talked; before Abba left, he'd lift me onto his lap and they'd laugh. Naeem. Butter boy. *I can eat you up*, he'd say, nuzzling my hair, my neck, until I ran, squealing.

Sometimes he came back and took us for walks, when the streets grew violet-quiet and everyone was scurrying back into their homes, and you could hear the propane tanks humming. Always my mother was so tired and gaunt—she used to cough into the end of her sari—and I remember after a while she did not go for those walks. More often, Abba came home from work early, holding a white paper bag stapled at the top, and then he would go into their bedroom where she lay resting, with her thin wrist across her eyes.

And then my amma was gone. I was five; I remember people, so many people in the flat, and I would move around the forest of their legs. My abba told me that for weeks I walked around the rooms, pressing my palm to doors, poking my head in our tiny rooms, calling for her.

"Amma?" I would cry. "Where are you?"

I climbed up on the sill, stared out at the empty street, sure I would see her stepping off a bicycle rickshaw, her round face lifting to me. Sometimes I squatted by the kitchen sink to look, puzzled, into the dank cave of pipes.

But she was not there.

And so I was left remembering only a few things about my mother: how her thin wrists settled on the top of my head. How she sang to me in my bath, when she poured the warm water, sleeked my hair down like a wriggling snake. None of this Auntie and Uncle did for me, when I went to live with them. They were not bad people. But they did not sing. Uncle was old; he kept his teeth in a glass at night. Auntie's feet were so dry they rasped like insects. Auntie and Uncle just waited. For the mail from America, with news of the next money transfer. For the news of my father's remarriage, to Munna, the girl they had found for him through Auntie's cousins in Elmhurst. And for the green card, so he could send for me.

Now I was seven. Still Before-Naeem. Still so good, in my school shorts and blue shirt, my smudged-ash knees that knocked together when a grown-up spoke. Uncle would bring me to his friends and he'd thrust me forward into their circle. *Listen to him!* he would boast proudly. *Father sends money so you go to English school. Show them what they've taught you!*

I shut my eyes, the sounds thrumming inside me. *How do you do, sir?* I said slowly, searching for each word. *I am from Bangladesh, sir!*

Uncle and his friends would enjoy this, their laughter tucking into their bellies. *Not bad. Soon you'll be in America with your family! Maybe on TV someday and we watch you!*

Every Sunday, Uncle and Auntie and I would crouch

18

over the computer Abba had paid for and Skype. His face floated up murky, and only once did I see my stepmother, Munna, before she moved off the edge of the screen. She looked shy, young. *Soon,* Abba kept telling me. *You will join us soon. I promise.* But one year passed, and another and another. First there was the delay with the visa. Then a baby was born—Zahir, my half brother. They were saving to take over a shop through a friend of a friend, in Jackson Heights. *Munna is overwhelmed,* Abba explained. *Next year.*

Instead Abba sent me postcards, of New York City, the Manhattan skyline, its buildings wedged against each other. "Manhattan, yes, it is very tight," he explained during our calls. "Streets are narrow, like Dhaka. But then you go to other places. So much space! One day I drive with my boss on a highway and I fall asleep for hours and still there is more highway!" I begged him to send me more cards, and so they arrived, showing places he'd never been to: the Grand Canyon, Yankee Stadium, the craggy Rockies.

Once he sent a big package of books that he'd found in a Dumpster at a house in Brooklyn where he was working on a renovation. *They throw away all the time here,* he wrote. *So much waste in this country!* Inside were glossy, flat books with colorful pictures I liked to flip through. My favorite book was about the planets—stapled into the center was a foldout poster I taped to my wall. At night the planets glowed blue, silver. I'd stare at the rings around Saturn, practice my English, feel the hum of vowels on my

19

tongue. In those days I was patient. I stayed calm. I knew one day, I too would be pitched far away, to a new continent, a new universe. Or tucked into a silvery building, high up, where my new family could begin.

I was eleven when I finally touched down on the ramp, my eyes sliding easy over the signs at JFK: INTERNATIONAL ARRIVALS. BAGGAGE. NON-U.S. RESIDENTS. I could barely sleep on the flight over; I was too excited. I didn't know that the blanket sealed in plastic was for me, or even the meal that came rattling on a cart on a plastic tray. I thought you had to buy everything, and I had no money. Until the lady next to me leaned over and whispered, *Your mother wouldn't be happy if you don't touch your food.*

When I got off the plane, I squared my narrow shoulders. I was brave. I knew what passport line to stand in. The man there, his name tag said Hernandez, and I tested it in my mouth. I liked how the *z* buzzed against my teeth.

"Not bad." He grinned. "You'll do well here, man." He knew I was Before-Naeem. Nice boy, reunited with his father.

What happened?

Was it the fright when I did see Abba—not in a photo, not on a hazy Skype screen—when I saw his sloping shoulders and thin gray hair, and that young girl beside him? She looked like my sister! In a purple shalwar kameez, a curly-haired boy hiked to her hip, waving frantically at me, as if they knew me. My heart shrank to a cold fruit pit. I did not

20

know these people. I did not know the true sound of my father's voice. The way his head did a shaky tilt to the right when he spoke. How he drove funny: one hand each at the bottom of the steering wheel, so the car jerked forward on the Van Wyck Expressway. He was a terrible driver, which made me ashamed.

At night, I lay in my new bed, under crisp sheets decorated with rocket ships, and tried to memorize pieces of him. I heard his gargle-cough through the thin wall. Then my stepmother murmuring as she massaged the small of his back—a bulging disc, the doctor had said. I tried and tried to make the pieces hold. But still he was not mine. We were not a family. Not really.

And then one night I heard a sound. Feet padding on the floor from across the room. It was my little brother, who had gotten out of his own bed and was standing over me. His eyes shone like buttons in the dark.

"Bhayia?" Zahir whispered. Brother.

He reached out and pressed a finger into my cheek, hard. As if to see if I was real. I smiled in the dark. Then he climbed back into bed. Ever since then, it's as if I can always feel the indent of his finger in my skin.

A month, a year, middle school, slid by. I learned the rhythms of Elmhurst and Corona and Jackson Heights. I was fast, too fast, in all the wrong ways. I was snapping slang out of my mouth, easy. I knew how to twist away from the teachers, how to use my backpack like a shield. I

simile

21

went to a nearby middle school and hung with a bottom-feeder crowd, the ones who put firecrackers in garbage cans and ran away. The ones who slouched in the back of class, forgot their algebra books, their marked-up essays.

Whenever the work got hard—when I landed in a tangle of questions I couldn't answer—I gave up. My stepmother tried to help me with my homework, pushing her finger down the page.

"It's boring!" I protested.

"Sometimes. But once you do the little things, it all starts to add up. Like here, just go over the verbs again—"

"No." I twisted away, tears swimming in my eyes. It was embarrassing, being tutored by my stepmother, who was only ten years older than me. Up close, I saw the mole at the side of her mouth. Her face is very round, like a pan, with a spray of freckles across her almond skin. *simile*

"Naeem," she urged. "You have to study. There's no other way."

"I'm fine, Amma. It'll work out. Really."

Sometimes they'd call Abba to school and he would stare at his shoes the whole time. "Do you want a translator?" the counselor would ask.

"No," he said at one of those meetings. As always, he kept his gaze on his shoes. I noticed a hole in the seam of one, which made me flush, angry.

After, on the way back home, Abba kept his head bowed. "*Jotha shaddo koro.* Do your best" is all he could say as he shuffled into his bedroom. "Don't make trouble."

In his eyes I could see that he didn't know what to do

with me. And I didn't know what to do with him. We had no words for who we were. Who we were becoming.

Near?

The text dings just as I'm at the bottom of the subway stairs. Up ahead, the noise and rush of Queens Boulevard.

There was one thing that Abba was right about: I love Queens. I love its smells, its layout. Maybe because it's so big and prairie-flat, that wild moody sky overhead. The blocks start to spread, stretching to all these other neighborhoods—Corona, Woodside, Flushing, Bayside. On and on the borough stretches. Northern Boulevard, past the frayed silver flags of the car dealers, the jagged skyline of Manhattan rises like some wrecked and far-off city, a jagged Kryptonite kingdom, comic-book surreal. All around, a shredded violet light, the sun's rays bouncing off the slow-moving bumpers. You can slide and dream in a landscape like this.

By eighth grade I learned to move fast. I could feel the energy thrumming electric in my veins. Like that broiling July day, everyone twitchy with heat, when me and my friend Jamal crashed the playground kiddie area. We knew we weren't wanted. There's a big sign on the kiddie fence that says ALL CHILDREN MUST BE ACCOMPANIED BY AN ADULT. We didn't care. Those sprinklers were streaming fans of cool water. The pavement glinted, hurt our eyes. As we loped through the gate, I saw the mothers tighten their hands on the stroller handles. We goofed around, splashing each

23

other, until our T-shirts and shorts were totally soaked. I saw myself through the mothers' eyes: Clumsy, too big. Trouble.

I began to change my look. No one thought I was Bangladeshi anyway. Some of the guys on the street called me *Niño* instead of Naeem. My jeans pooled around my sneakers; I had a new hiked-up bounce in my walk. One summer I kissed Renata by the empanada truck her uncle drove. Her brothers saw—Dominican guys with serious thick necks—but I was faster than them both; my orange-tipped Adidas flew me, hard, over the fence.

Niño, we'll get you.

They never did.

I was out of there, shaking myself loose. I didn't care where I went; I just knew that I had to keep moving. My earphones jammed in my ears, a few dollars in my pocket, and I swung myself up the elevated train stairs. Or I hopped a bus. I borrowed my little brother's beat-up bike and swung it down Roosevelt Avenue, pumped my knees till they burned, just like the Salvadoran delivery guys with the huge chains looped around their seats. I knew a lot of neighborhoods. Sunnyside, Elmhurst, Flushing, even down all the way to Richmond Hill, where I kissed a Guyanese girl under a basketball hoop.

I kept running. I was fly: winged high-tops, arrow-elbows. It's as if I were still five, pressing my palm against doors, trying to find that lost part of me somewhere.

Up the stairs, bumping past shoppers streaming down. My elbows flinch as I spot a burly security guard near the entrance. A part of me doesn't blame him for eyeing me. By high school I was doing stupid things. I went to a local high; the first two periods before homeroom could be wiped off your attendance, so I learned to dawdle a few corners away from school with my crew of guys.

I hopped a turnstile. Swiped gum, candy. My fingers twitched. That expensive silver-etched pen? It twirled into my pocket at the Staples store, I swear I don't know how. The lady took me by the elbow, steered me to a back room stacked high with cartons of printer cartridges. She wore a red polo shirt and tan pants, like all the employees. Her name tag said *Hi, I'm Donna!* She looked not much older than me.

"You realize we can have you arrested?" she asked.

"For a pen?" I asked, incredulous.

"Um, yeah!"

"Oh." So much for thinking I might ask for a job here. Mostly I felt stupid.

The next time it was a calculator. Calling to me at the Best Buy store. Beckoning, twinkling, with its padded buttons. All the fancy functions. I'd seen other kids swipe stuff now and then.

They called the cops this time. While I waited in a back room, I heard the scratch of the walkie-talkie in the hall outside. Their shoulders bumping against the wall. They were big, like football players, grinning as if they'd just scored a touchdown.

I shook so hard. It was the only time I've cried in front of strangers.

"You're a good kid," one of the cops said. He had a little sleek black device fastened to his belt. "You did a damn idiot thing."

I gulped down the spit lump in my throat.

"I messed up too when I was your age," the other one said. He stood with his legs apart, hands latched to his belt. He reminded me of the passport man, Hernandez. The one who saw me Before. Who knew I was good.

I mumbled, "Yes, please, sir. I am so sorry, sir."

They left me with a warning, nothing more. My name tapped into his little device.

CHAPTER 3

IBRAHIM'S IN THE MALL ENTRANCE, ROCKING BACK AND FORTH on his shoes. Toe, heel, toe, heel. He does that a lot lately. Something's jiggling loose in him.

I met Ibrahim spring of junior year one night, trying to sneak into a bhangra club. A guy I knew in science class had told me how to get a fake ID. Thought I'd give it a try. I'd never done anything like that; I stood in line, anxious, turning the plastic card in my palm, watching those NYU *desi* girls with their sleek black hair swishing past. They are mermaids, those girls, all spangle and glitter and haughty looks. I ache for them something awful.

The bouncer took one look at the card. His gold chain jiggled on his fat wrist.

"Don't insult me."

He didn't even give it back.

Behind me I heard a laugh. Then someone came twisting out the shadows. He was sucking down a Coke, tossed it to the curb. The metal scraped.

"Don't litter," I told him.

"Don't fake it."

We grinned at each other, as if recognizing a cousin, an old friend. This guy was skinny, too skinny, his black jeans held up around his hips with a leather belt. His chest was scooped hollow. And he had a few pimples by his jaw, like a regular teenager. Shaving rash, he told me later, but I liked him better, thinking he was goofy-young like me, still dabbing on Clearasil.

"I know of a party," he said. "Not far from here. My cousin's place. You can dance there too."

"Where?"

"Elmhurst."

"How do we get there?"

He shrugged again, pointed to a car. It was a taxi, a bona fide medallion taxi. The yellow pooled on the hood, almost blinded.

"You a driver?" I asked as I slid inside. I noticed a tiny Pakistani flag dangling from the rearview mirror.

"My dad's. He owns a fleet of them."

"For real?"

"Sure."

I knew it wasn't true. But I liked him for saying such a crazy thing, seeing if it would fly. This guy showed imagination, guts. That night we didn't even go to a party. We just drove around and talked.

Ibrahim began to pick me up after school. Before, when classes let out, my friend Jamal and our crew would hang on the corner until we had to go home or help our families. We'd waste time teasing the cute-hipped girls coming down the block, or go to the mall.

Then Ibrahim came driving right up to the corner, elbow over his door.

And he fed me all kinds of ideas. We'd park in one of the lots at Flushing Meadows Park, stare out at the lake. Ibrahim lit some weed, smoke curling sweet in our lungs, and we talked about all we could do. Acting. How I was going to model or go to California, audition for a reality show. How he had a friend who was a music producer.

"Yo, Ibrahim," I'd say. "You're spending too much time online. Get your head out of there."

But Ibrahim was always in his head. 'Cause everything to Ibrahim was a great, unfurling possibility: Gucci and Apple stores and pretty girls and sleek office buildings. Sometimes we'd walk the streets of Manhattan, Ibrahim leading the way. I saw everything through his hungry eyes. The doormen with their gold-tasseled uniforms, women with their long legs emerging from taxis. We weren't on the outside. We weren't two kids in scuffed sneakers standing on a curb, watching rich people go into clubs, blue beams slanting on the pavement. Because of him, I began to feel that the city could be mine.

"It doesn't matter," Ibrahim assured me, when my grades began to dip senior year and I was put on academic probation. "What about Bill Gates? He never finished college."

Yeah, right. He never finished *Harvard*.

Now, in the mall, Ibrahim seizes my arm. "You're late," he chides. "And we have a lot to do."

"We?" I shake him off. I don't like how he looks. Sallow. His pupils thin as filaments. Today he's dressed pretty nice, jeans creased, white oxford, open at the neck, a blue blazer, shiny loafers with no socks.

"I gotta buy a suit."

"A suit?"

He grins. "Interview."

I nod. Right. Like the McKinsey interview he dreamed up a few weeks ago. Said it was a summer internship, in the bag. When I asked about it later, at a taxi driver joint in the city, he dipped his kathi roll in chutney, crinkled his brow, and said, "It wasn't for me."

As we step into the mall, I crane my neck sideways to acknowledge the guard. It's always like this. In the dollar store I feel the manager at my back, like the smoky tail of an airplane exhaust. *Can I help you?* Always everyone is so helpful.

"Don't you have anything else to wear?" Ibrahim asks. "Do you always have to look like such a homeboy?"

"If I'd known this was a big deal—"

"Forget it." He waves a hand, showing the slender gold chain around his wrist. "We'll find a way to explain."

I've always known Ibrahim is a liar. He told me about his uncles—filthy rich, their gated compounds back in Lahore. Or his second cousin in Dubai, who he's engaged to. Or the job interviews he's got lined up through a friend of a friend. *Serious business consulting, man.* I knew none of it was true. Or was it? I liked that he played his roles so well he believed them. I can't do that.

When I challenged him, I'd see his lashes sweep down. He's so pale. He doesn't eat well or much. My stepmother saw him once and cried out, *"Beta,* come here right now and we put some decent food in you!" She didn't care that he was a Paki, like those dirty soldiers that did dirty things to her aunt. All that was behind us. We live in the free world now. The free world of New York City.

Why do I hang with someone who so baldly, so badly lies? Because I know that what falls from his mouth isn't true, but it sounds so good, so possible, which makes it almost true? Because he makes me, the son who breaks his parents' hearts daily, feel like gold? I think: *I can't be that bad. There's still hope. Finish the quarter and I can pull through on the grades. Do a year of community college. Then get into Queens College.*

Sometimes, stacked in the backseat of the car, I see his chemistry and marketing textbooks, still sealed into their plastic wrappers.

"I'm selling them back," he explains. "I didn't like the classes. Boring profs."

"What does your father say?" I ask.

He goes silent, steers us onto the wide swath of Queens Boulevard. We're the same that way. We like to move. We don't stay still long enough to say what hurts.

—●—

Ibrahim is four steps ahead of me, plunging past the makeup counters with those scary mask women, then down another escalator, to the men's department. He goes right to the area where they've got suits locked with a thick cable through the sleeve, and a guy has to shake them loose with a key.

"Would you like me to start a dressing room?" he asks. He's an old dude, heavy, stomach flopping over his belt, tired eyes, but I like him right away. I don't know why.

"Why not?"

"Important occasion?" he asks Ibrahim when he emerges from the dressing room with the suit on. The salesman settles the jacket on his shoulders, tugs down on the back flaps.

"Graduation. My father's coming in from Lahore." He checks his watch. "He told me to take care of it because he had to stop in Paris on business." He smiles. "His alma mater too. Columbia. His professors still remember him."

I shake my head. Ibrahim can't even keep his lies straight.

But the man is impressed. I've seen this before. With his ambiguous looks, Ibrahim can pretend he's many things, testing people. Sometimes he acts like he's the son of a rich Saudi—though he has to be careful these days, with all the nutty fears, and Fox TV. He did that once in a restaurant and the waitress got nervous, convinced he was on his cell for all the wrong reasons. She sent over the manager, who asked us to please pay the check and leave. We did.

As we walk to the mirror area, the lies keep unspooling. "I didn't even know about this mall," he continues. "What is it called, sir?"

"Queens Center."

"I'm in Manhattan. East Side. But since we were on our way to the airport, I told the driver to stop. To save time." His accent has gotten super posh. Ibrahim knows how to do that too.

He wags his head. "Forgive my friend here. I tell him to stop dressing as if he's a hoodlum. My family does have a reputation, after all. But it's a way of slumming, I suppose. They're all so affected by MTV. You should see my cousins, when we get together at the compound. The way they prance around. They think they're the next Beyoncé and Jay Z or Zayn Malik. Drives the elders mad."

The man smiles.

Now Ibrahim's standing on a low wood platform where there's a three-way mirror, and the man is brushing his shoulders. "Just remember," he says. "A suit like this, it can be used forever. A suit is an investment. Graduation. Interviews." He smiles. "Wedding, even."

I like this man even more now. He gets why we're here. It's not just a suit. It's Ibrahim, flashing back to him in a tunnel of possibilities. I think of his jeans crumpled on the floor in the stall, left behind.

"What do you think?" the man asks.

Ibrahim's grin is a mile wide. "I like it."

"Just remember we can tailor too." He pinches the back of the jacket. "I'd take this in, just a little."

"I agree," Ibrahim says.

I'm amazed. My friend, with the pimple-rash at his jaw, with the scooped-out chest, looks fine, spiffy as a rich man. No different from the ones he conjures up all the time.

33

Maybe he could be one of those guys he says he could be—McKinsey consultant. Investment banker, MBA, toeing his shiny Prada shoes onto the subway platform every morning. I see them sometimes when we head into Manhattan: *desi* guys just like us, bent over the *Wall Street Journal,* leather briefcase wedged like a blade between their ankles. Or that guy who comes into my parents' store all the time but never finds what he wants. Once I saw him on the subway platform, a cloth WNYC bag hanging from his shoulder. An ache swelled in my throat. I wanted to tap him on the elbow, ask him how to get there. To *be* him.

"The thing is—"

"Yes?"

Ibrahim pivots. "I can't really tell without a shirt. A real dress shirt, you know?"

The man nods vigorously, as if embarrassed that he didn't think of it himself. "I'll be right back, sir," he says.

I keep thinking Ibrahim is going to rip the suit off his body and we'll tear out of there, laughing. I keep waiting for him to give up the game. We've never kept it up this long. But instead he glances at the label on the cuff. "It's silk and wool," he says. "Joseph Abboud."

"Ibrahim," I hiss. "You can't buy that. For real, man."

He glares at me, because the man is back, sliding the cardboard from a folded-up shirt, shaking out creases. He's got a stack of others tucked under his elbow. "I brought a few so you can see the options. That suit's a great color. Charcoal. Goes with a lot." He suddenly slaps his hand against his head. "I forgot the ties! We've got some really interesting ones." He tosses the rest of the shirts onto an armchair. "I'll go get some."

Suddenly I feel sorry for the man. This area of the men's department is completely empty. Five o'clock in the middle of the week must not be prime time for suits. The only other customer is picking out socks. How often do you have someone at Queens Center checking out a seven-hundred-dollar suit?

"Hey," Ibrahim calls, "let my friend go with you. He's got a great eye."

The man smiles. "Sure."

As we're leaving, Ibrahim calls out, "Get a lot, Naeem. My dad really likes ties. I want to get one for him too."

My head is a sparkler, fizzing out with the absurdity of this scene. Here I am picking out ties for a job, a graduation, that doesn't even exist and for a father who, last I heard, owns a fleet of taxis and hates Ibrahim's guts. Or so I think. I can't keep any of this straight.

But me and the salesman, we're picking out ties as if it's the most normal thing in the world, as if he's some nice uncle helping me out. Our arms bump. We survey the ties, lined up in tucked rows.

What about this? He drapes the ties on his arm, expertly. I touch the slanted edges, admiring.

I could do this, I think. *I hear they take applications. Maybe apply tomorrow.*

By the time we're back in the dressing room, Ibrahim has put on the whole ensemble—pale blue shirt, suit—and we hand him my favorite tie, the one with maroon diagonal stripes. He looks elegant. I almost believe he's headed for a graduation.

"Listen," Ibrahim says, checking his watch again. It's a fake Rolex—he bought it off a Chinese guy jiggling them on a pole on the subway one night. "My dad gets into JFK just about now. How late are you open?"

"Nine o'clock."

"Perfect. Can you hold this under my name? We'll come right here, so he can see all this." He smiles sheepishly. "I can't really go ahead without his approval."

I can see the man is disappointed, but he quickly covers it up. "Of course."

The dressing room has shirts, ties tossed everywhere. The man is desperate to make a sale. So the trousers are shaken out just so, clamped into the bottom rod of a thick wooden hanger, the jacket over that, a little cardboard tag tied around the wire hook with a fake name and number. Three shirts and three ties too.

As Ibrahim and I leave the men's department, there's a strange pressure in my ears, like when I was on the airplane, a giddy whoosh in my stomach. We glide up the escalator, weirdly happy. I've never felt so light. Back on the ground floor, among the stands draped in bead necklaces, Ibrahim twists away from me. "Hey, listen, can you meet me in the front? I promised Ma I'd get her this perfume she likes. It's her birthday soon."

I shrug. "Sure."

I watch him weave toward the counters, melting into the other shoppers. My backpack hangs heavy on my shoulder, making my socket ache. I'd forgotten how full it was, having set it down on the dressing room floor. My math and physics textbooks are stowed in there—if I cram, I can clear the Fs. Get off academic probation. So I turn toward the mall entrance to wait for Ibrahim. Maybe after I can find a quiet spot at one of the food joints, put in a few hours.

It takes a few seconds for me to realize that the crazy bleating noise was triggered by me. The metal rods stationed at the entrance are flashing wild, for me. And the security guard and some woman in a cardigan are bearing down—on me. Then my arm is seized, the backpack yanked off my shoulder. I see the suit guy bringing up the rear, looking not uncle-like at all, but tense.

Shaking my head, I squint over the glass display cases, the other shoppers frozen, grim. I realize what was eerie-wrong before. I'd forgotten. The watching. The cameras, the clicks, the parked cars, the guards tracking my knees, my stupid-looking ears, my thoughts. I'd pretended me and Ibrahim, we were shaken loose, unseen.

Right there the woman zips open my backpack and the shirts spring out in a gorgeous fan—pink, blue, cream. "Where's your friend, your friend?" the salesman keeps asking. But I know. Ibrahim's in the air, free. He's gone. And me? I'm here.

All alone.

CHAPTER 4

"You want some water?"

The man shifts his legs, leans forward, pushes a Poland Spring bottle across the table. For a cop, this guy has treated me pretty well. Like a visitor, almost.

It's weird: when we arrived at the police station, I wasn't booked. Instead one of the cops leaned across the desk and talked softly to a woman. Someone else led me by the elbow, down a hall. They took my backpack, my phone, but that was it.

Now I'm in this room with no windows, rubbing the raw creases on my wrist, sitting across from a tall, lanky guy—Taylor, he says his name is—and he doesn't even have a uniform. A detective, I figure. What's to investigate? Pretty straightforward. Dumb high school senior stuffed three Ralph Lauren shirts into his backpack.

"My partner will be here soon," Taylor explains. "Won't be a minute. Go ahead, drink up."

I unscrew the bottle cap and suck down water. My throat burns, peppery-mad. *It wasn't me,* I want to say. *My friend! He's a pathological liar, a freak, and he does stuff like that.* They don't give me a chance. They just make me wait. Which is worse, in a way.

I still can't figure out what happened. The scene keeps looping in my mind: Ibrahim turning in front of the three-way mirror. Sending us for the ties. Did he know there wasn't a camera in the dressing room? That we'd meet back in the front mall, Woodhaven Boulevard's traffic teeming around us, and I'd hand him the shirts? Or did he want me caught?

Taylor looks at a folder, taps his knuckle against the tabletop, using a chunky school ring. He even smiles at me. "You're at Newtown High, right?"

"Yeah."

"I went to Van Buren. Played basketball for them. You play?"

"I shoot hoops. Play a little soccer. But nothing regular."

He shrugs, looks away. I feel as if I've disappointed him somehow. He goes back to tapping his ring, rhythmic. One, two. My own heart's jumping a scared beat.

No one has called my parents, which has me relieved and scared. Give it a few more hours, though, and my cell phone—wherever it is—will vibrate. My stepmother never texts. Says it mixes her up, that tiny screen. She will speak very softly, bewildered, so I can barely hear her. *Naeem, didn't you say you would come home by eight?* She never knows, exactly, how to be a mother to me. She speaks to me sometimes like a son, scolding, and sometimes as a brother.

The door swings open. Another guy strides in. Blue hoodie, Timberland boots. He's glaring. I can see ragged sweat stains beneath his armpits. Never mess with a man who's sweating a lot. He's already in a bad mood.

"So." He sits, flicks his eyes at me, as if already I've taken up too much of his time. "The store is ready to press charges. And the Staples incident will be used on setting bail. We're not talking juvenile court, of course. You're already eighteen."

"You know about that?" My throat is super parched, even though I've drained half the water in my bottle.

He tilts his forehead down, as if to say *Are you kidding?* He's heavyset, with a thick, scrunched brow, a coppery sheen to his skin. He reminds me of my gym teacher when I come up with some lame excuse as to why I didn't bring my shorts.

Flapping open the folder, he reads, rubbing his thumb on his lower lip. Then he squints at me. "Not doing well in school?"

There's a prickly sensation at the back of my neck. Just like that weird, pixelated feeling when I know I'm being tracked, in stores, on the streets. How could he know that? "What do you mean? I'm going to Queens College!" I blurt, jutting out my chin.

He smiles.

"I am!"

Taylor leans forward, sets his hand on my wrist. Mine looks so skinny under his broad palm. "Hey, hey. Calm down. I had a lousy GPA too. It's not the end of the world."

He gives me a reassuring smile, which washes me in confusion, then anger. I'm supposed to hate these guys. They're the ones Amma tells me to stay away from. Now here he's talking about high school basketball and GPAs! He's trying to fritz my circuits. I remember my cousin Taslima warning me about the cops: how they pick you up, spook you, take you to the station. A kid I know was two hours short on his community service and they pulled this bull. Stay cool.

But it's hard. Taylor is watching me with a careful gaze; the other guy—who hasn't even told me his name—has retreated into sullen silence. This is worse than if they had asked me questions, yelled, did all those mean and swaggering gestures they do on police shows. I sense him watching. Gauging. Every bit of my body, every hair, feels lit up, seen, bathed in an ultraviolet light. I'm a specimen of cold fear, twisting in their lab dish. I just want to scuttle away. Hide out, like my little brother under his mound of stuffed animals. The thought of Zahir gives me a stab of pain. What's he doing now? Sitting cross-legged in front of the TV. Wondering where I am.

"Okay, let's look at your options," the second one finally says. "We can take you down the hall and book you. I'd put my money on a conviction. They're really cracking down these days. Even on small infractions."

"But it was my friend who did it!"

"Yeah, right. That's original."

The men smile at each other. Burning, I stare down at my knuckles. He's just trying to scare me.

"And your parents, they can put up the bail?"

I don't answer.

"I thought so." He winds his fingers together. They're stubby, tough-looking. "Every time you fill out a job application, you'll have to say, *I was arrested for a misdemeanor.* I'll put my money on a conviction. That's even worse. Imagine explaining that for the rest of your life."

I don't say anything.

Taylor looks idly at the folder again. "Your parents. They came over here when?"

"My . . . father eleven years ago. My stepmother a long time ago." I add hopefully, "She went to school here."

"Their papers in order?"

A knot tightens in my stomach. "She's a citizen. My dad has a green card. We're okay."

"You sure?"

"Yes."

"You know any trouble on a green card it can be revoked, right?"

There's a thumping, deep as a bass, in my chest. "No. I didn't know." My voice is a lot smaller now.

"Here's the thing, Naeem." That's the other guy—Taylor. He seems concerned, his voice soothing. "There's another option."

I don't budge.

"Naeem, look at me."

I lift my head. I can see that Taylor is all neutral, pewter eyes and gray hair trimmed tight around his ears. Unlike the other guy, he wears a crisp white shirt, the sleeves neatly folded up above his elbow. I remember those shirts in Macy's. Three lousy shirts.

"We can have the charges dropped. Easy."

I feel a quiver of relief. "That would be great! I promise, I won't do it again. It was my friend—"

He puts a palm up. "We have a need."

"A need?" I swallow.

"For guys like you." He adds, "You can keep an eye on things in the neighborhood."

"Where?"

"The mosque."

My eyes swing between them, bewildered. "I don't go to the mosque," I mutter. "Not anymore. Not even my dad."

"That's okay. There's lots of other things you can do."

"Like?"

He glances at the folder. "Chat rooms. Friends. That's very helpful to us. Student groups. Muslim student associations."

"I don't join any of that stuff!" I protest. "I don't like politics."

He grins. "Even better."

I jam down in my seat. If I go very still, like a lizard that changes color, they'll lose sight of me. Forget I'm here. That's what I want. To not be seen. To not be so noticed.

I'm a loser, a kid who's wobbling through senior year. Just a smudge in their calculations. Close the folder, mister, please, and walk away. Let me go.

But the blue-hoodie guy is smiling at me. He scoots his chair a little closer, rubber tips skidding on the linoleum. His eyes are like small, moist figs. "My partner here thinks you're a good kid. I don't know, myself."

Taylor asks, "You know what we're asking you to do, right?"

I can hardly breathe now. My teeth hurt. This is a test, only this time, I'm not confused. I know exactly what he's asking of me.

Watcher.

Both men get up, as if on cue. Taylor's hand drops on my shoulder. It's warm, almost tender. "Come. We'll get you something to eat. You must be starving."

CHAPTER 5

WATCHER. MOSQUE CRAWLER.

Abba always looked forward to his time at the mosque, especially Friday-night prayers. That was when we fit snug, as best we could: my abba, my half brother Zahir. My stepmother stayed at home to pray and cook. Abba palmed on his skullcap, his long white kurta. He looked elegant. The seam threads glinted fine in the sun. We'd walk several blocks with Zahir, my little brother's hand light in mine. He was so sweet, so trusting. Sometimes Abba and I would hoist him up between us, let him swing high, until he gasped with laughter. We were good, then.

A few blocks before the mosque, Abba grew somber, quiet. Sometimes they set out a small speaker, the call to prayer rolling out into the street. You'd think it was the center of the universe, the way people came streaming out of buildings, off the stoops, palming on skullcaps, like my abba.

All around us a blue-black twilight lowered, the streets a dark river of frenzied action, everyone rushing home at the end of the week, picking up their dollar loaves, the Chinese ladies pushing carts of bruised vegetables the stores sell at the end of the day. We were a school of fish, going in a different direction, swimming toward this ugly building that used to be a senior center. I joined the others, kicked my sneakers off, washed my feet under the spigots, folded myself on the carpet. Then I'd dip my head down and dive inside, letting the prayers roll over and through me. After, it was like coming up for air, sun and shiny teeth, joking, regular talk. We joined the flow again. We'd stop for a few minutes, chatting with the men who hung around outside. Then Abba would take us for ices down the block—the drizzled, bright-colored cones sold by the Mexicans on Roosevelt Avenue. Zahir and I had a contest—who could gulp the ice down faster and not cry from the cold. We laughed so hard then, tears scalding our cheeks. We were ourselves, but changed somehow.

About a year ago, soon after the detectives came and asked questions at the store, we came out of the mosque blinking and Abba said, "We're not going anymore."

"But why?"

"We're not."

He jabbed a thumb in the air, did his shaky head-tilt. Even in the dark I could see the low outline of a car parked across the street, a blue Chevrolet. "You see that? Plain-clothes police. All the time." He shrugged. "I don't want any trouble. Store is hard enough as it is."

Crazy old man, I thought. Abba loves to stay up late and watch the American police shows, especially reruns of *Law & Order* or *Miami Vice*. He likes *The Good Wife,* though he doesn't approve of the character Kalinda's behavior— wearing her skirts too short and kissing both girls and boys.

So I checked it out for myself. The next day, after school, I looped around the block near the mosque. The car was still there. I could see the man's forearm, freckled, reddish hairs lit up in the sun. Mashed-up Dunkin' Donuts bags on the passenger side. I couldn't believe it. It was exciting, in a way.

I went back the next day: a different guy, same car. Same crumpled garbage tossed on the grooved rubber mat. I stood there, amazed by these shadow guys threading through our neighborhoods. Secret-agent men. How could we be so important? We'd been given some kind of celebrity status, but in all the wrong ways.

Then I felt a sharp nudge to my back. I whirled around to see the imam, brow furrowed. Boy, he was not happy.

"What are you doing here, Naeem?"

Shame flooded through me. "Just hanging. Messing around."

He pulled me across the street, so angry I could see his lip quiver, which it did when he took us boys aside for a scolding. "Do not joke like that. This is not funny. These men are serious."

I tried to rearrange my face, make it seem as if it were

no big deal. But inside I was pretty shook up. Maybe he was right. This wasn't a TV show or a comic book. "Sorry," I mumbled, and slunk away.

Soon Abba heard they'd put a camera right near the entrance to the mosque. Some community leaders complained, but the little boxy camera is still there, bolted to a telephone pole a few feet away, a black security insignia glinting like a tiny crow in the sun. My cousin Taslima, who runs a human rights group, walked around the neighborhood, trying to get people to come to a community workshop about what to do if an FBI man comes to your door. Some argued, said it's a good thing. "They are protecting us." Most nodded and turned away. Like Abba, they were frightened. As if they'd already been caught on film, overexposed, grainy.

"Come on, Uncle, we have to fight this," Taslima urged Abba when she stopped by his shop.

He shook his head, firm. "No fighting. We do not fight."

I knew what lay behind Abba's dimmed eyes, the stiff shoulders: the war that made Bangladesh. How his own older brother, Rasul, slipped away in the middle of the night with a rucksack to join the *Mukhti Bahini*, the Freedom Fighters, to fight Pakistani rule. *No more war*, Abba often said.

Now I swear I see cameras everywhere—on the street poles, clicking inside cars. And Abba, he rolls out his rug, prays in the back of the store. Sometimes he joins the men in the alley masjid, not far from our store. Not even for Ramadan did he go to the big mosque. When he goes to watch the soccer games in Flushing Meadows Park, he unfurls his rug on the grass, adjusts it under a tree just so, to make sure he's facing east. The bottoms of his feet are dusty, callused ovals. I'm proud and angry, watching him do his prayers, even as the guys from Ecuador are kicking a soccer ball nearby, or some white women are power-walking in their skimpy tank tops. I'm furious because he won't go back to the mosque. He lets himself be out here, on the scruffy lawn, the cars from the Grand Central Parkway thrumming past. His forehead has a leathery imprint, the shape of a thumb, from all his hard work to Allah. It's not the same, of course. That hole of calm we used to step through twice a week, it's shut tight now.

CHAPTER 6

"Tell me about yourself."

We're sitting at a diner in some neighborhood I don't recognize because we came by car, bumping down so many streets I got confused. Taylor is doing most of the talking, acting as if this is a regular job interview. The other guy—Sanchez, I've learned—stays out of it. He's busy dabbing his fries in ketchup, popping them into his mouth. "You like school?"

Outside, a light drizzle has started, and a pretty girl has paused to snap open her umbrella. She's wearing a raincoat, and she has to tilt a little, hold her arms out, to make the cheap handle work. For some reason, it hurts to see this. As if she's off-limits, as if I'll never be out on the Queens streets again, loose, doing what I want.

"Some. At first I thought maybe I could be an engineer. Finance. But forget college. The math is killing me." I remember with a pang the brochures Amma set down on the breakfast table.

"So what do you like to do?"

I shrug. "Acting and stuff."

"Really?" There's a trace of a smile around his mouth, showing his very straight teeth.

I nod. "I was Kenickie in *Grease*."

"I can see that," he laughs. "Not bad."

For a second, I flash on Ibrahim—Mr. Business Major— and a soreness scrapes up in my throat. He used to promise to be my manager. Or we'd watch YouTubes on his iPhone and he said he'd make a video with me. My hand flits to my pocket for my phone. Then I remember I've got nothing on me.

"When I was in high school," Taylor comments, "all I wanted to do was play basketball." He shakes three sugar packets into his coffee and stirs.

"That's not very healthy," I tell him.

He smiles. "You're observant."

I flush. "Sort of."

"That's what we need."

"Guys who keep their eyes on things," Sanchez adds. "That's how I got recruited."

I turn to Sanchez. He has me on edge—he seems to flash from bully to distant observer. Underneath I sense a boiling temper.

"Did you go to cop school?" I ask.

"Cop school." He grins. "I like that." He dabs a fry into his ketchup. "No, I went to ambush school."

I give him a puzzled look.

"Army. Deployed to Iraq two times, Afghanistan once."

"Oh. Wow."

"Saw a lot of stuff." He stares off through the plate-glass window. Now I can see lines running down his jaw, turning him older. "So now I do intelligence."

"In your hometown."

"Brooklyn. Grew up in the Red Hook projects. How'd you know?"

"It's easy." I point to his hand. "You've got a ring. A high school ring. Taylor's is Fordham. College. But you probably went right to the army, straight after high school?"

They try to hide it, but I can see the pleasure lighting both their faces.

"How'd you do that?" Sanchez asks.

"It's nothing." I shrug.

"No. Really. Tell us."

It's funny. For the first time I kind of relax. There aren't many people I can talk about acting with. My parents would freak. It's not a real job. "Drama class," I explain. "We do these character workups. We have to know everything. Like what they eat for breakfast. Or who punched them in the face in third grade. Stuff that isn't in the script." That's the longest string of sentences I've given these guys since this night started. I even feel good about it, and sink back in the booth.

"Go ahead," Sanchez says, crossing his arms across his chest. "Work me up."

Sanchez is all armor and heavy defense. I can imagine him in some massive tank, scanning a dangerous city. It's like he's still in that built-up vehicle, watching the world from heavy-lidded eyes. He's someone who doesn't trust, ever.

"You probably had a whole gang you ran with in the neighborhood," I try. "Got into some scrapes. Messed up. Then you thought the military might just do the trick. Secretly you kind of liked the cops who used to give you trouble. You admired them."

"Not bad!" Taylor elbows his partner. "What'd you think, Carlos? Got you pegged?"

Even Sanchez gives a grudging laugh. "You've got talent, kid. Where I come from, you run with that. Otherwise life has a way of running after you."

This may sound weird, but my spirits lift. This is the first time in months, maybe years, anyone has said something nice about me. Especially these last few months. And especially coming from Sanchez. I'm so used to being the one who disappoints. After-Naeem. Mr. Screw-Up.

"It's true," Taylor says. "There are things you can do with this. It's a job. Could even be a career."

I cough at that, incredulous.

"Seriously. You do well, you can take the exam. Maybe join the force. FBI. CIA. It's a great future."

"We can even help you with getting on track, college-wise," Sanchez adds. "You'll need money, right? Your dad, he's got a store? With this economy, I bet he's not doing so well."

"He's okay."

"There's money. Four, five hundred a month." He makes a bridge of his stubby fingers. "It can go up from there. Depending on how well you do. What you get for us."

I let this sink in. So they're serious.

"Hey, you haven't eaten." Taylor points to my plate.

It's true. I ordered a tuna on toast but have only managed to eat a couple of bites, the mayonnaise curdling sour in my belly.

Sanchez slides out of the booth and stands, hikes up his jeans. He's glowering, checking his watch, as if my little display never happened. His wrists are thick, strong, like his neck. I wonder if he wrestled when he was in high school. I should have put that in too.

"We should go." He looks down at me, irritated. Beneath his nylon Windbreaker, I can see a slight bulge. Doesn't take talent to know what that is.

It's thirty minutes later. We're sitting in their car, silent, with a view of a dingy subway entrance. My elbows stay tensed at my sides. I'm not sure what's next. Do they take me back to that room? Book me?

To my surprise, Taylor's handing my backpack to me. The zippers jingle a little. "Okay, kid."

"That's it?"

He shrugs.

54

"But what about—" I want to say, *the shoplifting charge? your offer? my talent?* An auto body and junk shop mounds across the street, broken shells of cars piled high behind a chain-link fence. "What's next?"

He grins. "You're good at that stuff. You'll figure it out."

"But—"

"Get going," Sanchez says in a low voice.

I slide out of the car, then hurry, shivering, too scared to do anything but move forward. Just as I'm stepping down the subway stairs, I glance back. But their car has vanished, melting into the night.

CHAPTER 7

THE NEXT DAY AT SCHOOL, IT'S LIKE I'M AN ASTRONAUT LANDING back on Earth. I've been to some weird planet I didn't even know existed. Whisked into a version of *The Matrix,* only to be dropped into first-period homeroom. I catch myself scanning the other kids—the homeboys slumped down low during English; the Dominican kids flicking their long combs through their flattops. They look so young, silly. How many of them have ever been in lockup? Eaten fries with detectives? I can't tell whether I'm weak or powerful, having this secret knowledge.

But it's Friday. I hate Fridays. That's the day when everything I've been avoiding piles up. A guilty ice-drift slowly leaks into my stomach. The essay I was supposed to turn in, the quiz I have to take, the science lab I meant to write up. It's the last quarter, and a trail of incompletes, no credits, and bad grades blots my transcript. It's not that I don't know this. It's that I don't know how to fight my way back.

Ten minutes into third period the loudspeaker blares and the secretary calls my name for a conference with Mrs. Delarosa. I hate that word. *Conference.* Makes it sound so important. But at this point in the school year everyone knows. Who is borderline. Who had his parents called in a few times.

"Mrs. D!" I say, trying to put on a grin as I saunter into her office and drop my backpack by the chair. I've done this before. It's not the first time I've been called.

Everyone loves Mrs. D. The girls cluster around her office at the end of the day, showing her their new shoes or nail polish, or she's always got a group of us joking around, since she runs the drama club. She likes to ruffle my gelled hair, teasing, *What's in here? Cement?*

Today, no smile. Her eyes look drawn, her lips chapped and pale. She's dressed for summer in a pretty sleeveless top—the color Amma likes, coral-pink—and it shows off her sunburned arms, her freckles.

"What's the matter?"

"Oh, Naeem." She shakes her head. "*Hijo,* what am I going to do with you?"

My jaw goes stiff. "What?"

"You think I'm stupid, *hijo?*" There's a bright flush on her cheeks.

Oh boy, I think. Mrs. D is going to launch into one of her outpourings, all in Spanish. She slides a folder across her messy desk. Inside is a printout of my most recent

57

grades. D in English. F in math. I wince. I know all this. I just don't like to look at it.

She points a finger. "Naeem, it's the fourth quarter. *Fourth* quarter!"

"I know."

"You remember when we met with your parents in the fall? I spent an hour with you all! We went over everything! We signed a contract. How you had to have no less than a C in all subjects by April fifteenth to graduate. Remember? We joked about how you and the IRS have a lot in common? Deadlines?"

Of course: we sat in the conference room just off this office. Abba looked stern and nervous—I could tell he understood about half of what Mrs. D was saying to him. And my stepmother, she kept translating, until Abba got annoyed and angry with her. He doesn't like it when she embarrasses him in front of strangers. His English isn't bad—he just didn't understand this whole "contract" business. It's a new get-tough policy at the school.

"What happened?"

"I sort of fell behind—"

"*Mijo!* Why didn't you call me? You get in trouble, you're supposed to call me. Not do this on your own."

Mrs. D wanted to be an actress herself—she's crazy and passionate about us all, especially the "second gens," as she calls us. "Caught-between babies," she likes to say. "And I catch you so you don't hurt yourselves."

Now she leans toward me. "You had to do the work! I promised your parents I would keep an eye on you!"

"I know, Mrs. D. But the quarter isn't over. Mrs. Reale, the math teacher. She likes me! She'll let me make it up."

"Naeem—"

"Seriously! She says I have nice teeth!" I try flashing her my megawatt smile. It's a stupid joke, I know, but usually Mrs. D laughs along with me, makes a few calls, and we work something out with the teachers.

"Naeem," she says softly. I feel awful. She's really upset—no act here. A strand of hair trails down her cheek. "Baby, you don't get it. You can't joke your way out of this mess. You should have seen her after class when you were confused about the tests. And why didn't you hand in your final essay?"

"I forgot." My hands are twisting between my knees.

All spring I've lied and dodged and run. After the meeting, I told my parents I was on top of my work. I didn't go to the math lab—I ducked past, embarrassed. I told myself I'd make it up the next quiz. Or we'd switch topics and I'd do better in that one. I made sure not to show my parents how they could log on to a computer and see all my grades. It would never occur to them. That's the crazy thing. I'm good with details. I remember everything when it comes to lying.

Senior year was starting to feel like an escalator: I could barely stand on the first lapping steps and they were gliding all the way up, up, to next year. The acceptances were pouring in for everyone else. Even Jamal, who used to goof around on the corner with me, cut classes, got into City College for engineering. Priya, a girl I used to crib off in math class, has a free ride to Hunter College. All I got was a provisional acceptance to community college if I keep up my average at a 2.5.

"You're too old for this nonsense, Naeem." Mrs. D sighs. "Really." She runs her fingers through her hair. "Maybe I am too."

"Mrs. D, seriously. I can do it. Just give me a chance."

An abrupt shake of her head. "Graduation is in six weeks. You know the drill. Grades have to be in two weeks before. We're less than a month away from that. Even if you were to do everything right—" She touches my wrist. "You understand what I'm saying? You can't graduate."

We sit there a few minutes, not saying anything. My whole body has gone numb. I'm angry. Then furious at myself.

"Listen up, *hijo*. Unfortunately, with the budget cuts, the make-up classes aren't running until the fall. There is a summer program, it's very good. Even better. You'll bang it out. Get this done with." She slides over the printout of my transcript, and a flyer: *High School Offerings at LaGuardia College. All Subjects.* I don't move. "There's a fee. But you only have to pay four hundred."

"So I can't walk?"

I can see her eyes open a bit in surprise; then they grow sad. She shakes her head. "I'm sorry, *hijo*. That's not possible."

Her eyes well up, green polished in wet. I can't stop wiping my own with my sleeve.

Mrs. D silently pushes a tissue box in my direction. I

don't take it. She blows her nose. The bell rings, but still I stay stuck to the chair. A thumping river of noise rushes past, students hurrying to their next class. Everyone on their way somewhere. Except me.

"What is it, *hijo*?"

"My parents—" I don't finish.

Mrs. D bites her chapped lips. "I'm so sorry, Naeem. Really. You have to tell them."

"But—"

"Do it tonight," she insists. "The school will notify them by letter. You don't want them finding out that way."

I can see Abba: The proud lift of his chin. How he worked so hard to master his own English. And here I couldn't finish a lousy essay! My backpack feels as if it weighs a million pounds. As I head heavily for the door, I hear her call, "You'll be okay, Naeem. It's just a setback. I have faith in you."

Then I see she's holding something out. It's the flyer for the summer school programs.

I float through the halls as if I've been socked in the stomach. I can't go to class. Not now. The bell lets out a bleating wail. The last of the kids filter into classrooms. Doors slam. A sheepish skinny kid flies out of the boys' bathroom, hiking up his jeans. Probably a freshman, sneakers banging, eager, on the metal stairs. That used to be me—scared, hopeful.

For a couple of minutes I think about flagging down

61

a friend. Jamal? No. It's been months since we've hung. A couple of the girls from *Grease*? No way. Not going to let them know what a loser I am.

I duck into a stairwell and push out through the side entrance, run down a side street, where the security guard won't catch sight of me. Outside the wind blows, stinging fresh.

Ibrahim? I keep seeing him turning in front of that mirror in the suit, a wash of light picking up silver threads in the fabric. The way he tugged down the sleeves, lifted his chin, pleased. I've seen that shine in his eyes before: a filament of excitement, a dare. Usually it ignited in me too. This was our secret code. Like the time we hung out in Washington Square and told two undergraduate girls we were talent scouts, looking for extras. I loved that. The unpredictability of him. Never knowing.

But that night at the mall, something was off. His skin sallow. Sweat coated his brow. And his eyes too shiny. The last I saw of Ibrahim, threading his way to the makeup counters, vanishing. What the—?

I text Amma, tell her I'm studying in the library. I just want to disappear into the jumble of Queens neighborhoods. I get on a bus, all the streets I know skimming past: Forest Park, where I watch kids shoot hoops and sometimes join in, though I'm no good. Now the yellow buses are lumbering down streets, disgorging kids at stops where their parents or grandparents wait. I'm watching my earlier life, a slow-motion loop, a disaster. I feel old, weary. All the excuses, the small lies. What did they get me?

Early evening is crumbling from the sky by the time I make it back to my neighborhood. I pause at the old playground. The last of the kids are straggling home, dragging plastic buckets and balls and scooters. Lights prick on in the surrounding apartment buildings. A few boys linger in the baseball area, their bats cracking balls into the dusk. But soon they are gone. I imagine all the families setting out dinner plates inside apartments, kids bent over homework. My heart hurts; I wish I could follow them, press the magic button. The one that lets me whisk back to that earlier time.

I sit on a swing, its seat hugging my thighs. A dull ache spreads through my bones. The air folds cool and dark around me. It's as if I can see him—Before-Naeem, with his funny ears that stick out from his head—arcing high, high, over this playground.

There's a shout, then a figure moving blurrily toward me. I squint in the fading air. Ibrahim?

"Naeem?"

But no, it's Taylor. The hair on his arms glows silver. And I can't help it: seeing him, my chest gives a tiny skip, both happy and nervous.

"Hey, why the sorry look? You're not glad to see me?"

"Not exactly."

"I'm used to it."

Then I see that tank of a guy, Sanchez, leaning against the fence, thick-shouldered, hard. My mood drops. Taylor signals with his fingers for him to stay back. Smiling, he comes toward me, sits on the other swing and moves gently, chains creaking.

I scowl. "Why are you following me?"

He shrugs. "Just checking things out in the neighborhood. Thought I'd see how you're doing."

"Yeah, well, I'm fine. Just fine." I spit these last words out.

"You don't look fine."

I don't say anything.

"Bad day?"

I try to stay quiet. If I just wait—for the dark to close in around us, for him to get bored with me and realize I have nothing to offer, for Sanchez to lose his temper—they'll leave me alone. Tell his buddies at the station house I'm a waste of time. But strangely enough, I like having Taylor here. He reminds me of a couple of the counselors I knew from YMCA camp a few summers ago. Missionary kids, fresh from Colorado, Utah. Even though we'd make fun of them all the time—especially the girls, with their moony expressions, their fresh-shaven, athletic legs, their braids with silly ribbons—they had a way about them. As if the world were a lot cleaner, brighter. As if there were nothing ahead to worry about.

"School? Parents?" He grins. "Girl?"

I sigh. "School." A stone pushes up sharp in my throat. "I may not graduate."

He lets out a whistle. "That's tough."

"I knew it was happening. Just didn't—"

"It catches up with you, what you haven't taken care of. Can't fake what you never did."

We sit in silence for a while, swings creaking. He can't see, in the dim and lowering light, that my eyes are wet. Back and forth we shift in the worn seats; my mood calms. I realize what I miss: Ibrahim. I'm sore and mad at him, but lonely too. I have no one to tell all this stuff to. In the old days I'd text him and tell him about the business with Mrs. D. Flaky as he is, he'd drive up and we'd go for a spin. I liked that I didn't see him that often. I'd unload what was fastened inside my chest. He was outside of things. That's what made it easier.

"Come on." Taylor is standing now and I can see he's wearing Converse, which shine like oblong boats against the dark asphalt. He points to the basketball hoop. "Wanna shoot?"

"I don't play. Not like you."

"That's okay."

Before I can object, he's hustled back to his car, which is parked by the curb. Sanchez hasn't moved this whole time. Taylor has brought a basketball, nestled against his hip. The streetlamps are turned on, casting a gray-hued circle under the hoop, enough to see.

We play one-on-one. It doesn't take a genius to realize this guy is good. His defense is strong and thick, like he's five guys at once. He elbows, he thrusts his arms in my face, lunges and steals. "Play to the left, play to the left!" he keeps yelling.

I give it a try, but I'm wildly off, my shot rattling the backboard.

"Take your time, Naeem," he instructs. "Bend your knees. Your wrist. Follow through."

We start up again and he loosens our range—we're not just playing right under the hoop for layups, but wider, working on three-pointers. Now I see his real talent. He is definitely point guard, feeding, guiding me, setting me up for a better spot. My shot sucks anyway, wilting off the side of the hoop.

He spins to a stop. He's panting hard, wipes his sweat-greasy face with his T-shirt collar. "You're not keeping your eye on it," he says.

"Sorry," I mumble.

"Don't be sorry. Just do it."

I reach for the ball, but he cradles it away from me. "You going to tell your parents? About not graduating?"

I shrug.

"You are, right?" The ball's still held just up over his right shoulder. I could smack it out of his hands if I wanted to. But his eyes glitter, furious.

"Yes," I breathe.

He shoves the ball so hard, the air is scooped from my ribs. Then we're back in—he tries to block, but this time I weave to the left. Let my wrist go, just so. Follow through. The ball spins once, luminous as a planet. The rim wobbles. And it drops right in.

CHAPTER 8

By THE TIME I GET HOME, SWEATY AND TIRED, ABBA AND AMMA are still at the store, doing inventory. It's my job to take care of Zahir when they're too busy—warming the fish fry and rice in the microwave, watching over his multiplication tables, making him take a bath.

Zahir's a good kid. Even though he's nine, he still sleeps with mounds of stuffed animals and plays with Lego on the floor for hours. Every day I see him march off to school with his Spider-Man backpack, a regular little soldier— straight, careful, chin tipped at what's ahead. Sometimes the others make fun of him—he's little for his age, with a funny, awkward air. He's good at math—taught himself how to add and subtract double-digit numbers in his head. He could go somewhere, unlike me. He doesn't care what other kids think about him. He only cares what I think.

"Do you like this Lego bridge I made, Naeem?" he'll ask, his voice catching with excitement.

"What about my report on Sandy Koufax? Did you read it, Naeem? Did you?"

I don't know why he wants so much from me. Maybe because Abba is too old for both of us, too distracted with the store and its worries. Maybe because, to him, I was a miracle: an older brother who just showed up one day, poof, stepping out of an airplane.

Zahir is obsessed with Spider-Man, even though he's getting a little old for that stuff—the thick red and blue cups, the huge stickers on our bedroom wall, Spider-Man ready to pounce, the ribbed pajamas with plastic eyes that haze in and out. He's the kind of kid who reads things over and over again, has perfect recall. He can tell me about cartilage in sharks; he corrected the science museum docents on the name of a man-eating plant in the Amazon.

He likes to come up to me at night, soft and tangy shampoo-smelling, and bring me his prized book—a hardcover Spider-Man, the old-fashioned one that tells the original story of Peter Parker. Even though he can read it himself, he makes me do it. He draws up his knees, laces his fingers around his ankles, shuts his eyes, and listens. It's as if we can both see them: superheroes, with their bright pop colors, their avenging missions.

"Naeem," he will say wonderingly. "You know Peter Parker lived in Forest Hills, Queens. Right near us."

"Yes, I know."

His smile is dreamy. "If I went to Forest Hills High School, I'd see him. I'd know who Peter Parker is."

"Yes, you would."

"Maybe I'd be in that science lab. The one with the radioactive spider. That made him powerful."

"Do you really think that's real?" I ask. His eyes are open, trusting.

"There are special cells," he explains. "They absorbed the radioactivity. They go through his bloodstream, even his heart, especially the aorta. That's why it's so effective." Zahir used to pore over an old illustrated book on the body I bought for a dollar on the street. Now I can see, he's wobbling between believing in Spider-Man's special powers and his own crazy, factual head.

After Zahir goes to bed, I sit at the kitchen table, my stomach twisted raw, waiting for my parents to come home. I'm back to feeling bruised, shaky, as if someone has knocked me hard in the ribs. Taylor is right. Tell them.

The key scrapes in the lock and my parents shuffle in, looking worn, preoccupied. Amma sets down the crinkly glazed plastic bag she uses for groceries she gets half price, when the shops close. Before I can say a word, Abba drops down in the La-Z-Boy. He doesn't even bother to go in the bedroom and change into his favorite lungi, as he always does, the fabric washed so many times I can see its pale white threads.

"What's wrong?" I ask.

He shakes his head. "Not enough for new supplies. Maybe we go one, two months."

I can hear my stepmother at the sink, the hiss and spray of water on a pot. "I tell your father, we have to sell different things. New things. Maybe for kitchen. The shop up the block, he has only junk."

He's shaking his head. "It's too late. We can't buy more stock. We need more money."

He looks at me expectantly. I know what he means. We've talked about me getting another job, not at the store, to help out, especially in the summer. Duane Reade, KFC. Anything.

My stomach cinches tighter, remembering Mrs. D, getting caught at the mall. My time with Taylor. I take a breath. Start with Mrs. D. That's easiest.

"Abba—" I begin.

He glances up.

"About school. You remember when we had that meeting with the counselor?"

"Yes, she's a very nice lady."

As usual, Abba speaks to me in Bangla, slightly formal, and I answer in English, or a mix.

"So about those classes—"

He beams. "You told me your English teacher liked your essay."

"She did. But I forgot to hand in the final one." I pause. "There's other stuff too."

He shakes his head. "*Ami bujhte parchi na.* I don't understand. What are you saying?"

It takes me a while to push the words out. My life these days is so many complicated excuses, all dense together, I have to pull out the one string I can be honest about. "Here's the thing, Abba." I say quietly, "It looks like I'm not going to graduate—"

I don't even finish. I don't have to. His face goes ashen. Then he makes that spit-sound of disgust at the back of his throat. "Throw it away!" he cries. "You throw everything away!"

"Yes, Abba—"

"I should have known! It is always this way with you! Everything I give you, you throw away! Treat it like it's nothing!"

I feel awful. My whole body throbs. "No, Abba. It's not like that. I can take summer classes. There are second chances—"

"Second chance? What kind of second chance do you have? I have? I came here with nothing and I work all the time. I hurt my back and still I must work. No such thing! Your mother, she had no second chance!"

Without a word, he rises, shunts his feet into his slippers. They slap at the backs of his heels as he stalks off, into the bedroom. The door slams shut. He might as well have squashed me right there, the same way he briskly breaks down cartons in his shop. In the silence, I can hear him loud and clear: *That's all you can be. All you are, lousy firstborn.* She kono kajre noye. *Good for nothing.*

Amma, who was listening in, starts to cry, saying it is her fault, she hasn't done a good job as my stepmother.

71

"School is mother's job," she keeps whispering. Soon she has gone into the bedroom too.

It's then I see Zahir hovering in the doorway, staring at me, wide-eyed. My head surges with heat. I pick up his plastic Spider-Man cup from the coffee table. "You're too old for this!" I yell, hurling it across the room. It bounces on the TV, rolls to the rug. His thin shoulders shake.

"Sorry!" I blurt out.

It's too late. Zahir just gives me those trustful sad eyes. That feels the worst. Zahir's watching hurts the most.

CHAPTER 9

THE NEXT TUESDAY, WHY AM I NOT SURPRISED TO FIND TAYLOR with his car idling two blocks away from school? As if we're best friends. Why can't I stop my chest from rattling like it's a paper cup, a tiny stone dancing inside? He brightens me up somehow. And why can't I stop myself from feeling that I *want* to see him? A rush of questions: Is he married? How old are his kids? Does he play ball with them?

No text from Ibrahim. None. A-hole. The shock of what he did is starting to fade. What's left is a slow-burning fury. A hurt that claws. I almost delete his number. Almost.

Ibrahim *has* been off lately. Showed up with glazed eyes, as if he'd spent too much time online. No car. Said it was in the shop, but it was weeks, maybe months. Sat in the diner, nursing his coffee for an hour. One day he showed me a stapled pamphlet. The kind given out by those black dudes in robes selling incense, saying the world is coming to an end.

"You look like crap," Taylor says as I walk over to the car. Today he's back in his Oxford shirt look, pale hair silvering his arms.

"I feel that way."

"Rough time?"

"Yeah. I told my parents. Like you told me to."

"Come on." Taylor pats the front seat. "You need a little sustenance. Then we'll take a look around."

He's not alone. Sanchez is in the back, hunched against a door. He looks as unhappy to see me as I am to set eyes on him.

"Where?"

"I'll show you."

I glance over my shoulder. My parents will be worried. Or maybe they won't. Ever since I told them about graduation, there's been a deep freeze. Abba isn't talking to me. Not all weekend, even when I unloaded cartons and flattened the cardboard, even when I spent a couple of hours with Zahir making a Lego castle and then taking him for ice cream after. None of it helped. Maybe they're glad when I'm gone. Out of their way.

"Okay," I agree.

We don't talk much, which I like. Not a peep from Sanchez. Even better. Taylor drives with one hand resting on the wheel. He's got a fancy watch, not like the fake one that Ibrahim bought off the Chinese subway guy. You can tell by the gold—it's not cheesy yellow, but a deep rich color—

what Amma eyes in the Indian jewelry shops on Seventy-Fourth Street but can never afford. Taylor's got taste, class. He didn't drop a crumb when we ate, sleeves cuffed just so. Doesn't talk unless he has to. Doesn't need to prove himself.

I like this kind of moving. Soon we're skimming along the West Side Highway in Manhattan. Tall, old-fashioned buildings on my right; to my left runs the Hudson River, small whitecaps ruffling the surface, a low cluster of buildings in Jersey. For a couple of years now Abba's been talking about moving to Jersey—Paterson, where the store rents are cheaper. Maybe get a real little house, some yard for Zahir. Somehow they never get ahead enough to make it happen.

In front of us rise the towers of the George Washington Bridge; for a second panic flutters in my throat. Is he taking me across? Then we're circling off a ramp and steering down narrow streets, where people are straggling out onto the front stoops, in front of the stores, or leaning on cars.

Taylor parks where a cluster of teenage boys gathered just outside a deli. A couple of them clutch beer bottles in paper bags; others are just smoking. He turns off the ignition, cups the keys in his hand.

"Come on. I need to pick up some fruit."

To my surprise, I like following Taylor. He's cool, appraising. His gray eyes tick off everything: the guys on the corner, from their sneakers to their hoodies, fists stuffed into their pockets; the crumpled bag someone tosses into a garbage bin. He's moving as if this neighborhood, this whole city is his court. He can glide on its polished surface, sink a ball when he wants. Even when he's buying a bag of grapes from the vendor on the corner, I can see how he keeps a part of himself detached, observing.

"I see kids like that all the time." He jabs a thumb at the group on the corner. "That one, he's been in for a year. Or that one, goofing around? Tells me he's going to get his GED. You know where they'll all wind up?"

"Where?"

"The usual. Flipping burgers. Working for some moving company. In jail with a girlfriend hounding them for child support." He adds, "Is that what your parents brought you here for?"

I stiffen, press my shoulder blades back. Lectures bounce off my mind like dull coins. Then I remember Mrs. D, her chapped lips and wet eyes. Me and my friends, we used to hang on the corner near the high school like these guys, idling, not sure what to do. Lorenzo dropped out before senior year. Feroze got in trouble for fights. Were we so different?

I'm relieved we don't go anywhere just yet—we sit on a bench and watch some other guys play pickup on a court. Their shoulders shine with sweat; their feet blur on the pavement. Taylor's watching closely. "A lot of kids, they go for the easy stuff. Want to be heroes."

I laugh. "Like my little brother. He's big into Spider-Man."

"Nice."

"Yeah. He's great."

Relaxing, he stretches his arm across the back of the bench. "Hero," he muses. "What's that mean? There's a lot about being a hero that's really chill. It's not the big, flashy stuff."

I nod.

"Invisible. That's the best kind."

A light drizzle starts and suddenly Taylor's up, gazing at me with those steel-gray eyes. I feel cold and warm at the same time. And I wish, for some crazy reason, he'd just brush his hand on my shoulder. Just once.

Now we're parked in Woodside. The rain is heavy, beading on the windshield; it's like being sunk in a submarine. I'll never get out of here. Never step out of our crummy elevator and see my family's shoes neatly lined up by the mat, or hear Amma calling to my father over the spray of dishwater. These guys have me. They may even drag me back to the station house, book me for real this time.

The worst part is that moment between me and Taylor is gone. When we returned to the car, Sanchez sat in the front seat, with shaved head, his mocking grin. "Missed you."

I gave him a curt nod, slid into the back, and we took off. The traffic was a sluggish drip down East River Drive, Sanchez popping grapes into his mouth the whole time.

"How come we're here?" I ask.

"The Heights, that's our old beat."

"And now?"

Sanchez swivels around. "Now we get to hang in my neck of the woods. Bay Ridge. Flatbush. And yours too. Corona. Flushing."

A wet, clammy dread spreads through my stomach. The air in here is too close, smelling of damp carpet and the grapes Sanchez polished off. I know what they mean: The Muslim neighborhoods. The kebab houses. Mosques. Little shops, like my parents'.

Taylor and Sanchez have grown alert, intent on a figure that's hurrying across the pavement in the drenching rain. We're across from a low clutch of small stores that slope down the street in a saggy row: a Chinese restaurant, a hair salon, a real estate agent, and an electronics place.

"See that kid?"

Through the bleary glass, I can see a boy breaking down cartons by the curb, kicking them flat. He looks to be about my age. Black hair cropped close, almond-colored skin.

"His name is Omar," Taylor explains. "He works in his uncle's shop. Took a trip to Yemen last year. Recently he's had some interesting activity online." He points to a door I didn't notice before, leading to the second floor, where there's a sign that reads CYBER CITY. MONEYGRAMS. INTERNET CAFÉ. "That's where he does his business."

"That doesn't mean anything!"

Sanchez turns to me, as if anticipating this. "Of course it doesn't. But we can't be too sure, can we?"

"But that's—"

"Profiling?" he says.

I hunch deeper in the backseat, furious.

78

Taylor bends toward me, speaking in that soothing voice. "Look, that's where you come in, buddy. You can tell the difference, right? Between just a little playing around on a site? And someone interested in the real thing."

"This is crazy!" I burst out. "This stuff doesn't go on. It's just made up, from TV and the news and—"

"How can we know?"

"You can! I can just tell—"

My words hang there, like an arrow that's met its target, air vibrating, feather quivering. *Ding*. Of course. That's what they want me to say. *I can tell*. The boy has since gone in, drawing his hood up over his head and dashing inside. I'm glad for him. I can't stand our gaze on him, greasy with need.

Taylor says, "You're smarter than you let on, Naeem. You've got real skill. You're observant. You catch things. Like that whole acting bit. Stuff doesn't go by you. That's why we like you. You can join a team. Be part of something bigger."

"Bigger?"

"You'll be feeding us information to send on to the unit. Not many kids your age get to be part of such an operation." He says this as if he's recruiting me for basketball.

"What if they find out?" I ask quietly.

"Who?"

"My friends. My family."

He grins broadly. "That won't happen, will it?"

I feel as if I'm going to throw up. I think about Thirty-Seventh Avenue, how I can see every one of those shops—the

79

dosa place and paan seller, the men on the corners selling religious books and prayer rugs. The Mexican guys who sit on crates in the back of the bigger outfits, shaking dirt out of the spinach leaves. Or the girls over at the waxing and threading salon, who tease me all the time about my hair. How could I sell them out?

And this kid, breaking down cardboard out front. That could be me, doing the same for my parents. What's the difference?

But maybe not. Maybe that day when I walked over and stared at the detective, I opened a door. I didn't want to stay crouched, hidden. Me and Ibrahim standing outside some restaurant watching people eat twenty-dollar salads, wanting *in*.

Why not? Abdul, son of a friend of Abba's, joined the force. I see him sometimes, strolling down the block, hands on his holster. Every time we hear about a terrorist attack, we all feel it: the dread and surging nausea. Abba stares at the TV, his eyes wet. "This is no religion," he mutters. For days after, we walk around shaky, hushed. As if even the air could bruise.

I can change that. Abba no longer in the slant of shadow, fearful, wary. No one asking questions at the store, frightening him. Money.

We don't move. We don't stir. The bag of grapes is crumpled on the floor. The rain finally stops, leaving slick streaks on the windows.

"So what do you think, Naeem?" Taylor asks softly.

I can't answer. My eyes drill down to the carpet under my feet.

His voice is low, soothing. "You want to turn your life around?"

A rustling noise up front. When I lift my head, I see it's Sanchez, wearing a stupid grin. I feel sick; I want to heave onto the carpet.

This is the moment Sanchez has been waiting for. In his fingers: a little plastic baggy with my weed.

"I found this the other day. In your backpack." He massages the thick plastic, showing the weed I sometimes keep in there, the stuff I got from Ibrahim. "What do we have here? Not just a dime bag, huh?"

My throat's gone tight as a straw. I can hardly breathe.

"Shoplifting is nothing. But this—" He shakes the bag once more. The dried leaves and seeds jiggle. "More than a dime bag." He tips his head. "And with shoplifting too."

"Not good." Taylor.

At that moment, I realize this isn't a choice. Not really. If I say no, I'm back to the station house, where I'm just another Queens kid with goofy ears and a lousy high school transcript, pressing his thumbs on ink. Not for shoplifting, either. Possession. No small thing. I'm the failure son, calling Abba, his face worse than before, lines of grief running down his cheeks. Amma in the back of the store, silently crying.

It's a test. Multiple choices. Like Ibrahim tilting in that three-way mirror, selves flashing back in a Joseph

Abboud suit, silk-smooth, fine. I can see a different self walking down Seventy-Fourth Street, shouldering past the cop. Loose, easy, in the know. Just like Taylor. Professional. Gauging, noticing. I can feel my college ID in my pocket. Handing over the crisp bills to my father—twenty, sixty, four hundred, five hundred. New spice grinders and pots stacked up in their store.

"Naeem?" Taylor whispers.

I look at him, my insides pulpy raw. He's broken my heart. He's smashed me into hundreds of pieces and put me back, so I'm glued to him. He knows that. I know that too.

He doesn't even have to ask.

It's two hours later when I step outside, the light embryonic, pale. The rain has rinsed the streets clean. My knees are spongy-weak; my eyes can barely filter the signs. I don't even know what neighborhood I'm in. A thousand years have passed. I've been in the Bat Cave; I've been abducted by aliens, sent back down to earth, Queens.

The streetlamps click on. I test my walk, as if navigating an ice patch, make my way to a bodega. I scan the shelves, choose a bottle of Snapple. At the counter, I check out the cashier. Her iPhone sits tilted on the counter as she combs through Facebook. The lit screen gives her face a bluish tone.

I see this hole-in-the-wall through their eyes: the phone cards they sell for five, ten bucks. "You know about that place?" I point to the worn stair leading up to a travel agency.

She looks puzzled, pushes the Snapple toward me. "Why?"

"Nothing." I feel stupid. I was just practicing; I don't really know what I'm doing.

As I step outside, up ahead, I can see the elevated 7 line, a new train threading past, the windows checkered yellow.

Now I understand about the magic of Before and After, poof. The passport man, Hernandez, he understood. *You'll do well here,* he said, as if I were already a made-over kid. And that's what I did. For a while.

But this is better. You make a mistake. Like Peter Parker, you touch the radioactive spider. You become web-footed, springy-fast, reaching into other people's lives. I can part the way, like Taylor. I slide out my MetroCard, hustle up the stairs like everyone else. From here, I can see the tops of buildings, right into other people's windows. A girl is turning on a faucet. Soon I'll do so much more. The train arrives, doors sliding open.

I step into the car. I am a watcher now. And I am new.

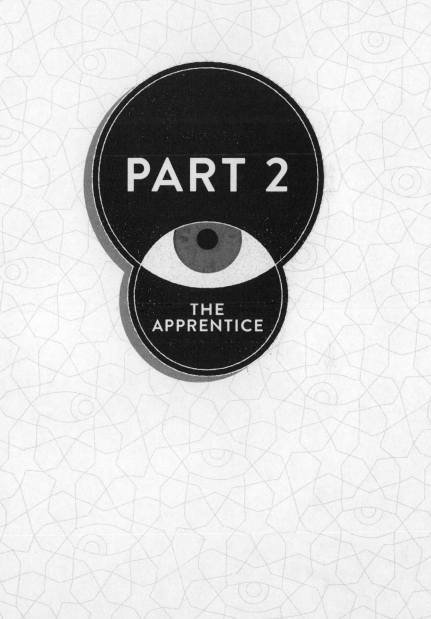

PART 2

THE
APPRENTICE

FILE

Subject: Muslim Youth United Conference
Address: Queens College
Approximately two hundred in attendance (list attached)

Locations

- Conference scheduled for 6/22 from 10:30 a.m. to
  4:30 p.m. MYUC has in the past had discussion groups
  of Kitab At-Tawheed. Has also brought speakers who are
  members of radical groups.
- Of note Yousef Kased at previous conference. He mentioned
  that he traveled to Saudi Arabia recently.
- Two students of Yemeni background discussed recent trips
  to Yemen.

Vehicle Information

Make: _____
Model: _____
Year: _____
Color: _____
Body Style: _____
Plate # _____
State: _____
(e.g., 4-door, 2-door)

- List attached.

CHAPTER 10

I BARELY SLEEP THE NIGHT BEFORE MY FIRST OFFICIAL MEETING with Taylor.

All night, I turn, sweaty sheets corkscrewing around me as it really hits me, what I've agreed to do. I feel like a tuning fork; the slightest touch vibrates, shocks me awake. The streetlamp right outside the bedroom blinds burns in a furry orb. I keep looking over at the mound of Zahir, worried that I'm keeping him up. But he's fastened tight into his dreams—one hand fisting his blanket, the other arm flung off the side of the bed, tender wrist turned up.

What are dreams? They are voyages, movement. We are superheroes, all of us; our skin glows. We have magic spines. We are Captain America: put in a capsule, waking as someone else, with new muscles. This is what I want: to feel instant change. The scales of my body shimmering, magnetic.

But the morning of my meeting with Taylor is nothing like that. I wake to a dark room, drawing fretful breaths.

These last weeks of school have been rough. We're in that start-and-stop time of exams and half days, everyone wilting down to the finish line. I've tried to block out all the talk about graduation and parties. I'm not going to the ceremony, of course. Amma's special shalwar stays in the closet, green-blue and glimmering like a frozen waterfall. Abba barely speaks to me, except to give orders about taking out the store garbage or stacking the newspapers. I just swallow it down. I'll make it up to them. I will.

Now it's early morning and the streets seem scrubbed raw, like me. A hard light facets the storefronts. The half-moons of dirt under my fingernails scraped clean. My cheeks sting from shaving so close, and from the Ralph Lauren cologne I bought on the street once for Abba.

"That you, Naeem?"

I turn around. To my surprise, it's my old friend Jamal. He looks the same: hair in a 'fro that makes him look like a skinny dandelion puff.

"What are you doing here?" I ask.

"Got a job a few blocks away. Rebuilding computers." He gives a sheepish smile.

It figures. That's what Jamal did all the time, in his parents' basement. He's so good at that stuff, that's why he got into an engineering school.

"You?"

I flinch, just a little. "Gotta meet someone."

His eyes slide around me, like he's trying to fill in the

picture of the friend who disappeared on him. I remember once, when Ibrahim came and picked me up, he asked, "That kid your friend?"

"Sometimes," I replied.

"Funny-looking dude."

"He's okay." I'd felt a swipe of guilt. But after that, it's like I couldn't go back to Jamal. I know he wondered what happened, why I dropped him like that. But I couldn't explain it. And there are some things you can't go back to.

Now he checks his iPhone. "I should go. My boss clocks me."

"Yeah."

It's a weird thing about friends: who's on top, who's on the bottom. Used to be I definitely thought I had it over on Jamal on the coolness scale. But now, watching him head down the block to his new job, with that little hike to his step, it's me who feels smaller, left behind.

Taylor's sitting at a table, already drinking a café con leche. I slide in opposite him. Out of the corner of my eye, I see Sanchez, perched on a stool, head tilted, ready to dive into a quivering slab of flan. This is getting to be our little dance. Taylor on me. Sanchez like a spurned girl, always within earshot. I get it. Teams. Cops. How they do business. Keeps me on edge.

"Hey," I say, trying out a smile.

"Hey."

I feel suddenly shy. It's as if it's my first day of school

and I'm not sure what to do. His gray eyes flicker, once, toward me, then at the Spanish telenovela on TV. "You want some coffee?"

I shrug. "Sure."

Taylor is different today. The guy who smiled when I swished into the hoop in the playground, who coaxed me into the car a few weeks ago, has vanished. Now he's a by-the-book detective, all business, cool, shut. I've noticed this before: the part of him that can withdraw to a compartment and then watch. I never know which one I'm getting. But maybe this is part of the training. I sit up a little straighter, wait for my cue.

Finally he talks. "Look. A job like this, you have to show initiative. We're depending on you. You're our eyes and ears. You understand?"

"I guess."

"Just guess?"

I wince. "No. I mean, yeah, I can do that."

He doesn't look convinced. A small panic pulses in me. I thought this was all decided. I had the job, easy. But now it's as if this is still a job interview. I've got to crisp myself up. "I know a lot of people," I offer. "I get around. Really."

He calls the girl behind the counter over. She smiles warmly, as if she knows him, and I notice he gives his order in Spanish. Damn, this guy is smooth.

I've barely finished my coffee when he stands. "Let's go."

"Where?"

An impatient look crosses his face. "Some sites."

"But—"

"Come on."

Why is he so tense? My stomach hurts. I didn't realize until now how much I want to please Taylor, show him I can be counted on, that I'm good at this. I can be like him. Detached, observant. Cool and chill. In the car I squeeze my fists on the seat belt. *Don't screw up.*

We pull up beside a low-slung building. Nothing special: Laundromat, discount store, brooms bristling out of rubber garbage containers. A Chinese shop where they sell funky-smelling herbs and concoctions in brown jars. But it's the Internet café on the second floor he's pointing to. Every step is seamed with scuffed metal, painted a different color, the centers worn.

"You know how much money laundering went on there?"

"What do you know," I breathe.

The window, which is crowded with signs for phone cards, MoneyGrams, transferring funds, is like dozens I've seen before. When our computer broke and we couldn't afford another, Abba used a place on Seventy-Third Street to Skype every week with my uncle. But through Taylor's eyes, it's as if everything is turning paper thin, decals blowing off to reveal something murky, not right, on the inside.

He reaches into his wallet and pulls out ten dollars. "Go in there, sign up for an hour. Take a look around, see who's there. Spend no more than thirty minutes. Note

93

everything—who's sitting at what station. What website they're on. If they leave, switch computers and see if you can get in there and see their search history."

I swallow. "Now?"

"Yes."

Behind the counter a man is thumbing through a newspaper. Urdu, I think, so he must be Pakistani. There are only two guys sitting at the stations—one an older man in a long white kurta and a sweater vest, even though it's warm out. He's smiling, chuckling to himself as he coasts the mouse to scan through family pictures—mostly kids. A wedding somewhere. Then there's a young guy in a blue hoodie and basketball sneakers. He's hunched in a way that I can't see his screen.

I slide into the next cubicle and log on, spend some time making new email accounts. CaptnA, I call one. Ahmed718 another. But I don't feel slick or fish-fly or magnetic. My fingers bang clumsily on the keyboard. I edge my chair back, catch a glimpse of the screen over the young guy's screen. Facebook. He's messaging with someone, tapping furiously.

There's a twitching motion and the other guy looks up. "Wanna give me some room?"

I scrape my chair back. "Yeah, sure. Sorry."

The rest of my session doesn't go much better. The next thing I know the man from the counter is looking belligerently at my screen. "Done with session?"

"Yes, sir."

"That didn't go so well," I tell Taylor as I slide into the

front seat. There's an anxious gnawing in my stomach. I'm sure he's going to fire me on the spot. I'm not a watcher. I'm a failure again. A punk kid who needs four hundred dollars for summer school.

To my surprise, Sanchez, sitting in the back, laughs. "Weird, huh?"

I swivel toward him. His voice is friendly, open. "Yeah."

"That's okay. It's always like that in the beginning."

Taylor puts a bill in my palm, folded. It's a fifty, and a piece of paper with all the sites he wants me to track.

Later that afternoon I pick up Zahir from school, take him to his karate lessons and then back to the store, where I help my parents do some stocking. We work side by side, silent, pushing the new bottles to the back of the fridge. The fifty-dollar bill is burning in my pocket. Not much. And if I can't step it up, my grand plan will collapse.

When I finally head back to the apartment and snap on the computer, I'm surprised at how easy it is. It's like dipping a toe, then a leg, then all of me, into a mercury lake. The air closes shut around me. Soon I'm in deep. The keyboard clacks. The lies shimmer.

Soaked in the blue light-waves of the computer, I test out my first screen name in an Islam support group. *I'm Ahmed, a business student at Baruch.*

Hi, the moderator says. *Exams tough?*

Yes, I reply. *Sometimes I think if I could figure out my praying and my studying, I could do better.*

That's why we're here.

I talk about classes. *Statistics nearly killed me!* About video games. About the Quran, how I was always lousy at memorizing. I know if you jump right into the far-out talk, everyone will freak and figure out you're a plant.

After a while, I'm feeling so smooth I venture to my other account, CaptnA. One click. Another, the soft leap into a new Yahoo group, this one about politics in the Middle East. I hang on the edges, take notes on who's saying what. It's nothing new. The usual mouthing off about crappy dictators and crappier regimes.

At some point, Zahir pads into the room, smiling sheepishly, his pajamas drooping on his bare feet. I notice the colorful pages of a comic tucked into his vocabulary workbook. He has his sly secrets too, reading under the covers, the flashlight turning his face pink.

"Naeem?" he says hopefully.

After Ma and Abba have gone to bed, Zahir and I like to stay up, talking comic books. The Marvel universe. The new series. Who's turning vigilante, who's working on the government side.

"Not tonight, Zahir," I say, smiling. "Tomorrow, for sure."

He climbs into bed, shuts out his Mets lamp. The apartment settles. Abba in the bathroom, then Amma. Pipes groan. I don't move. I'm lost in a new dimension, and by the end of the night, dry-eyed, exhausted, I've got five names to keep an eye on.

Today in my parents' store, the Starbucks guy's got on a wrinkled linen jacket with a black T-shirt underneath. I want to ask him what he does for a living, dressed like that, but he's browsing the shelves, impatient. "Pens?" he asks. We've got a few old ones in a box, next to the Tylenol packets that are probably expired, so I thrust out a Bic. He shakes his head, pulls out his own: slender and silver, the click kind. "You don't have any of these?"

I shake my head.

"Too bad."

Then he strides outside. Not even Tic Tacs this time. I almost want to run after him. Instead, I check my phone. I'm supposed to meet Taylor, give him an update. And hopefully get paid. It's been a few weeks on this Internet work.

"Not bad," Taylor says when I fill him in. We're meeting at a different bakery. Sanchez is in the booth too, dressed in one of those cotton shirts with an embroidered pocket and panel scrolled with pale blue threads. Dude looks like he's ready for Sunday fishing.

I can't complain. This time they let me drink my café con leche halfway before they set down what's next. "I was talking to my colleagues. Even this guy." He elbows Sanchez. "We have a good feeling about you. We want to give you more responsibility. More on-the-ground stuff."

"Why me?" I shake my head.

"We can use kids like you. You blend more. You speak Bangla, right?"

"Yeah. Though I forget a lot." A part of me is flattered. Isn't this what I wanted? But this sudden shift makes me nervous. I knew I would have to do more. I just didn't think it would happen so fast. Besides, I like the Internet work. These past few weeks, especially with everyone heading toward new stuff, it's my secret place. Now I can be someone else and no one knows.

"We need you to focus on some campus groups. Pay attention to political arguments. What speakers are invited. We're looking for names. Especially those who seem to be outliers. Expressing stronger views. Radical ideas."

"Where?"

"We want you to start with Queens College," he says.

"Queens College," I repeat, the word tinny in my mouth.

"There's a human rights group. It's run by someone who's not even a student. Graduated a while ago, but she convinced the administration to give her space. Her name is Taslima. You know her?"

A prickling sensation breaks out on the back of my neck. His eyes are on me, plain and serious. Was this a setup? I wonder. Did he know she's my cousin?

Taslima. Rebel girl. I used to love to hear all the stories about Taslima: how, when she was in college, she sneaked out on the fire escape at night, stuffing her clothes into her backpack and putting on a tank and cutoffs to meet her boyfriend. Last time I saw her was when she came by about her workshop.

"You have a problem with that?" Sanchez asks.

"No. It's just . . ." I have to hold down the trembling in my voice. My fingers grasp the sides of my coffee cup, as if to steady me. "We're related."

His gaze slides sideways. "If you're not ready, we can drop it."

That closed-in Taylor, the one who is just a handler and I'm a small-bit prospect, has returned. He's fingering his cell phone. I can sense his interest shifting elsewhere.

"No, no!"

"Seriously. We can keep you on smaller stuff. Some Internet places." He adds, with a small, tilted smile, "Not as much money in that. Won't get you noticed."

Noticed. That's another one of those words, bait, wriggly-smooth, tempting. "I can do it."

"You sure?"

I swallow, set the cup down. My hand shakes so hard coffee sloshes into the saucer. "Yes," I breathe.

We don't say anything for a while. My fingers slowly come ungripped from my cup. Taylor orders us three sweet buns, which we wolf down. Then he explains why they're targeting Taslima: how she's been holding a lot of events, outreach to mosques. I keep folding the idea over and over in my mind, like a piece of paper, until it's creased and familiar. "What do I do exactly?"

He nods, almost cracks a smile. "This is what we call 'cultivation.'"

Cultivation. He lets the word hang there. A door glides

open. His eyes have a bright, metallic sheen. I get the feeling this is what he likes most about this work.

"So how does it work?" I try the word out. "Cultivation?"

"It takes skill. You strike up a conversation. Show interest in their ideas." He laughs. "People love to talk. Especially about themselves."

I get the feeling that Taylor finds this a kind of weakness in others. He's hammered shut, and this is strength, to let others do all the talking. I make note of the way he holds his head set back on his shoulders so he can scan the room, me, the steaming coffee. I try the same, thrusting myself backward in my chair. A puff of air widens between us. That's what it takes. Don't engage too much, get riled up. Just observe.

"Get names. Pictures, if you can." He taps my iPhone, which sits diagonally between us. "Especially if they belong to the Muslim Student Association."

I almost want to laugh. My cousin isn't going to be any help on the MSA. Taslima hates those guys. She told me long ago. Says it's run by a bunch of old-school sexist know-it-alls who don't let the girls talk. "Want us all like their mothers," she scoffed. "We're supposed to bring the samosas and stay quiet."

"But what good is she?" I ask. "She's not even in an Islamic group."

"It's about connections, Naeem." Sanchez is talking now. "That's how information works. One group, one name, leads you to another. Look for buzzwords. *Jihad. Revolu-*

tion. This is a human rights group, and sometimes"—he laughs—"they get carried away with themselves."

"And the pay? For doing this?" I've surprised myself that I asked so bluntly. But I'm calculating: if I go to Queens College tomorrow and they pay me by the end of the week, then at least I'll have enough to register for my classes. I'll do English over the summer. Then make-up math, for the next session, in the fall. That still leaves some for my parents. Start community college in January.

"Get me some real leads." He tosses a crumpled ten-dollar bill onto the Formica table.

My mood drops. I thought I was on the *in*. In training. In the know. In with *him*. My jaw hurts, hard.

"And then?"

He sets his hand on my shoulder. To my surprise, it's warm, firm. I see a crease of concern. I feel stupid and ashamed at once.

"You show us you're making inroads and we'll talk about your compensation, okay?"

I nod, swallowing.

"You'll do good, Naeem. I know it," he says softly.

Then, with Sanchez offering a few silky Spanish words to the girl behind the counter, they're gone, the glass door flashing behind them.

CHAPTER 11

THE NEXT DAY IS HOT, HOTTER THAN I'D LIKE. BY THE TIME I make my way off the bus and up the campus and find the student union, my T-shirt is soaked through, pasted to my skin. I'm excited, seeing some of the pretty sand-colored buildings with their terra-cotta roofs, a green lawn, and sloping paths. This is where I hoped to go someday. Then I remember why I'm here. My iPhone is nestled in my pocket. I still don't know how I'm going to do this. Taslima is whip-smart, with a fast mouth. She's the one with the real X-ray vision—how am I going to escape her detection? My whole plan seems a joke—like some little kid's crayoned drawing, announcing: *Look at me! Mr. Super Agent!*

I find her group downstairs, all the way down a narrow passage at the very back of the building, next to a bulletin board littered with flyers. *Cheap Buses to Boston!* beside *Know Your Rights! Silence = Death*. Inside, the air-conditioning is turned off, leaving the room stuffy. Folding chairs are stacked on both sides of the wall, and on the floor are piles of paper and folders, clearly waiting to be stapled and put together. Taslima sits behind a desk, tapping urgently on her laptop.

"Hey!" she calls out, jumping up from the desk. Her eyes have that slightly cross-eyed look from too much screen time. "Look who's here! What's up?"

I shrug. "Staying out of trouble."

"Really. You, Naeem?"

I keep staring at Taslima. She's skinny and flat-chested as a boy, wears jeans that are probably two sizes smaller than mine, and ratty canvas slippers that the old Chinese ladies wear.

"So can I help?"

She squints. "You sure you want to?"

"Yeah." I shrug. "Thought I'd come by, see what I could do."

"Really?" She puts a fist on her hip, skeptical.

Does she know already? Then I remember: It's a job. A role. Don't act too eager—that will draw out her suspicions. Play it goofy and aloof. Taslima's no dummy.

"If you really want to know," I say, leaning close, "Abba just wants me to stay busy. He's not too happy with me these days."

"I heard. You flunked out?"

I puff my chest out a little. "I'm going to summer school."

She steps back in irritation. "I thought so. You didn't come here blazing with ideals. We're supposed to keep you out of trouble? Report back to Uncle at the end of the summer?"

I give her a sheepish smile. This is easier than I thought.

"Okay, so no babysitting here. Got it? We've got a huge number of programs lined up. I don't have time to train you." She waves a hand over at the floor. "Put those packets together. It's pretty obvious how to do it."

"Thanks, Taslima."

She's already behind her desk. "It's nothing." Her voice is gruff.

Before I squat on the floor and start assembling her packets, I snatch a glance at Taslima. There's a haggard, sad look drawing down in her eyes. She's blinking away tears. Her jaw is rigid. I've seen her look this way before. A lot of family and friends don't accept her. She's the shaming fire on everyone's tongues. Not just because she lied to her parents or did things on the side, like going to parties or having boyfriends. Because she flaunted herself. No one forgave her for that. Especially when she split with her parents, broke their hearts. They went back to Bangladesh, what with all the trouble after 9/11.

Taslima's so loyal to everyone, but her life is also somewhere else, off a foreign edge. Divorced, living on her own in some small apartment on Kissena Boulevard. No family, no husband. This group is her family. She rarely shows up at weddings or for holidays. But that doesn't stop people from calling her for a favor—an immigration problem, a contact for their kid. It's like they don't see Taslima—they see what they need, not what she's become.

The afternoon crawls along, me stuffing papers into folders. Not many people come by, maybe because who would want to spend a sweaty June afternoon in a basement office, making up packets for a workshop? A Sikh kid walks in from the South Asian Club down the hall and wants to borrow a stapler. I don't pull out my phone—nothing to photograph. I'm about to give up when Taslima is standing over me, a sheaf of flyers in her hand. "I'm dying in here, I need a drink. Want to come?"

"Sure." I stumble to my feet and struggle to keep up with Taslima, who's dashing down the hall, up the stairs, and over to the student union. She gets black tea with milk—as if she needs more caffeine to charge her up. We sit outside, under an umbrella, while she impatiently dunks her tea bag in her cup.

"So why do you do it?" I ask.

"What?"

"Help out so many people. And all that mosque stuff. I mean, you're not into any of that. They're kind of—"

"You mean they're jerks to me?"

I tense. "Yes."

She looks off, into the distance, her chin tipped upward. I can't tell what she's staring at. I keep searching for that girl who chopped her hair into an angry slant, who dared and rebelled. But Taslima's not like that anymore. Something has gone hard in her, like a thick leather hide. She married her boyfriend and then they got divorced. Now she barricades herself behind her meetings and placards and tables.

"You keep your eyes on the result, that's what I always say." But she doesn't sound so convinced. There's a husky sadness running under her voice, same as that look I saw in the office.

A girl is making her way toward us at the table, her expression brightening as she nears Taslima. She's carrying what look to be accounting books. She's nice-looking, with fair skin and a round, open face framed by a bright blue head scarf. Probably not Bangladeshi.

"Are you coming on Tuesday?" she asks Taslima.

"Have they agreed to give me thirty minutes?"

"I made them agree!" she giggles. The faint smell of soap drifts off her skin.

Taslima nods. "Okay, then." She swivels to me. "Naeem, meet Ishrat. She's willing to work with those guys over at Muslim Student Association. She's much more patient than I am."

Ishrat dips her head, blushes. Those eyes—startling seagreen, sparkling, too clear. They remind me of the smooth chunks of glass Zahir would collect at Rockaway Beach. They set me off a little, make me anxious. "They're not so bad." Then she adds, to me, softly, "You should come."

106

"Forget about him. He's just putting in time for the family. He'll be back to his Xbox as soon as they don't care anymore."

"I'll come," I say.

Taslima slings me a *Yeah, right* look.

"I will!" I laugh.

Excited, Ishrat fumbles with her flyer and hands it to me. I notice a tiny mole just above her mouth. "That would be great. We're having a youth conference on Saturday. A lot of great speakers are coming. An imam from the UK, even—"

A vibration starts in me; my bones tune in, expectant. The air under the umbrella has a new sheen. It's like one of those moments when you pull the lever down on those old-fashioned machines and you win—all the gumballs, the little toys in plastic bubbles, come gliding down the chute to you. I'm giddy, hungry to grab what I can. Everything glints, bounces with light, possibility. "Sounds cool. If you want, I can help out. Lifting boxes, whatever."

"Really?"

"Why not?" I grin. "I do it all the time for my parents."

I can see Taslima smirking in the background. After Ishrat leaves, she remarks, "It's because you like her, isn't it?"

I shrug. Even with those eyes, Ishrat seems bland, too student-government for me. It's everything else she said—*conference, speakers*—that's got me humming, alert. "She's pretty."

"I thought so. You don't fool me."

Saturday morning I'm up early. Both my parents are still here, which surprises me. Weekends are busiest in Jackson Heights, when all the families come in from other parts of Queens, New Jersey, Connecticut, Long Island, to do their shopping. From my closet I dig out one of my long kurtas and put it on over jeans. I never do that on regular days— only for family events. It feels weird. But when I look at myself in the mirror, I like what I see: my hair combed back with gel, a little mustache and goatee starting to grow in. Maybe I'll let it stay.

"What is this?" my stepmother asks when I come into the kitchen. She tries to hide the pleasure in her voice. My father is busy leafing through a newspaper, ignoring me.

I give her my usual noncommittal shoulder movement. "Nothing."

"Where are you going?"

I show her the flyer for the conference. "I heard about this, thought I'd check it out. That okay?"

"You see this!" Amma says to my father and sets it down next to his elbow. Poor Amma. Always trying to be the peacemaker.

"You are going with friend?" she asks hopefully. "Ibrahim?"

I start. Amma met Ibrahim once when he came by the shop. She liked the way he offered to hold the door and carry her bags home, which she waved away, laughing. "I am too young for this!" But she was pleased, color showing at her throat. That's Ibrahim. Knows how to work it on the outside. Who knows what's going on inside.

"No. I'm going alone."

"And where is Ibrahim these days?"

"I don't know, Ma."

It's been six weeks since the incident at the mall. I can still see him turning in that three-way mirror, a wash of yellow store light on his slender face. Later his shoulders pushing away from me, toward the makeup counters. Was that a joke? Something he did on impulse? Ibrahim was like that. Sometimes we'd ride the subway, and it drove me crazy, the way his leg would bounce up and down. *Cut it out, man,* I'd say. *It's weird.* He'd jerk his head back, embarrassed.

When I get to Queens College and see three guys, one with a skullcap, walk through the swinging doors, I almost lose my nerve. What am I thinking? All these MSA folks, they'll know I'm not the real deal. They volunteer, or talk about the ways they do good. They *care.* How am I going to fake that?

Taylor doesn't get it. I'm as much on the outside as he is. Abba had hoped I'd achieve Hafiz, memorizing all the verses of the Quran. I never got through more than a few. The few times I've tried, I felt exposed. Dirty, dingy inside. Nothing pure here.

Then I see someone waving to me from behind a table.

"Hey!" It's Ishrat, waving heartily, looking kind of silly and clumsy. Her long green tunic and turquoise head scarf bring out the color of her eyes. They startle me a little.

"I'm so glad you came! Taslima was sure you wouldn't."

"What does she know." I grin.

Her face goes pink. I feel bad and confused by how easy it is to tease her. It gives me a strange, dizzy power that I like and don't like.

"Would you mind taking over the men's table? The guy who was supposed to come called in sick."

Soon the participants start streaming in and I can barely keep up, checking names off the list, counting out bills, handing out programs. Malik at Baruch, business major. Syed at Queens, marketing. Mo, also at Queens. All the guys I've been compared to my whole life. They've got accounting and law books stacked up on their windowsills at home; they glide up the escalators at Hunter or Baruch. All of them are in college, on their way.

The lobby goes quiet, just like after the morning rush at my parents' store. I'm all alone. I relax. I can hear the muffled sound of the speakers inside. Quickly, I slide out my phone, set the registration pages on the table, and press. *Click*. Another page, *click*. Four in all. It's smooth-swift, faster than I would have thought. Thrilling, even. When break time comes, I offer to take a few pictures. I perch in the front row for the next speaker, snap some of him and the audience. Ishrat gives me a grateful look. The edges of her pupils, I notice, have a touch of gold. My stomach flops over. I can't tell if I'm glad this is so easy or dismayed.

That afternoon, when I join one of the workshops, is when the shift begins. I start to know what I'm doing. It's like putting myself through a door and realizing it's made of melting glass. It's not so hard. You can step right through and be on the other side. Your shoulders, your arms are made of putty. You are stronger, more flexible than you think.

The best thing about being one of the kids at the back of the room is you're already a spy. You know how to fake it. The other guys who are poking their hands in the air, involved, could never do what I can. I've got all the moves, the feints and angles. I know how to rearrange my face, make it attentive. How to slant my body, use my arm to hide my phone. Half listen while a camera coolly spools inside my head. For the first time, what I'm good at—lying with my body—has power.

I'm in; I'm so far in.

It's late by the time I get to a party at the Hassans', a graduation celebration for Ahmed, a kid I knew from way back, though he went to Stuyvesant, the top high school in the city. His mother once told my parents that Ahmed studied so hard for his entrance exam that his hair fell out. What kind of mother boasts about that? I guess it was worth it, since we're celebrating tonight—his graduation, his scholarship to Carnegie Mellon.

I should be pissed, but I've got six fifties folded into my pocket. Taylor gave them to me an hour ago, sitting in his car under the elevated tracks. "Not bad," he said. "Keep it up."

My family is already there. The apartment is packed—a tumbling narrow stream of shoes and sandals reaches all the way down the corridor to their door. Inside, the furniture has been pushed to the walls, cushions and sheets laid out on the floor. But even that's not enough room for the many people crowded inside. Mrs. Hassan is moving around the guests, happily giving out paper plates piled high with food. I don't see Ahmed, which is something of a relief, because then I would have to congratulate him.

I see my father with the other men, sitting on the floor, one leg drawn up, lost in talk. I freeze. I don't want to go there. I'm afraid of the hurt and anger that will pulse toward me like an electric current, and everyone else will see.

But then he waves me over, like a command. Next to him is Farouk Uncle, who owns a chain of pharmacies. "And what is next for you, Naeem?" he asks.

I feel my stomach tense and flex, remembering what Abba said this morning. "Taking a class this summer," I say.

He gives a nod of approval. "*Bhalo*. You are majoring in?"

"Still figuring that out, Uncle."

I go in search of my stepmother. She's not in the kitchen, where a lot of the women are doling out steaming food into the big foil containers. Nor is she in another room, which has been done up for the women, sheet and cushions spread on the floor. Where is she? Down a hall smelling too tartly of perfume, I find a darkened bedroom. This is where the purses and any jackets people brought are piled up on the mammoth-sized bed. Everything here is too big for the room: the walnut dresser, the tables, probably bought on some special. Two children are curled up asleep, their legs tangled in pocketbook straps and pillows.

And then I see. Through a sliding glass door, a tiny balcony with a purple bicycle locked to the rail. And a slender shadow: my stepmother.

My chest stirs. It's sometimes hard to see Amma by herself. When I see her this way, I'm always a little shocked, because it's then that I see how young she is. When she's next to my father, she's my stepmother, bugging me, setting down plates of fish curry and rutis or emptying out Zahir's backpack. But when she's alone like this, a little cord tugs loose in me.

"Hey, Amma," I whisper.

She turns. Her eyes are shiny-wet. Is she crying? "How come you're here?"

"I don't know," she says, shrugging. "So crowded and hot in there."

We stand, quiet. A soft breeze is blowing; I feel it on my elbows. The day's heat is starting to ease up. It's a nice, velvet-air night. She adjusts the dupatta on her flushed neck.

When she does start to talk, to my surprise, she doesn't say anything about how this isn't my graduation we're celebrating. "I am remembering when I graduated," she murmurs. "My parents, they too had party." She giggles. "They invited everybody!

"It was so great. They gave me tickets to see *The Lion*

King. I had never been to Broadway! Never took a subway by myself with my girlfriend!"

She smiles slyly. "At that party, they told me about my marriage, they had taken care of it. I was so surprised. They had two gifts for me. I did not know this."

I start; this is actually the first time I've heard this story. "Were you . . . disappointed?"

She shakes her head. "I was so happy. Everything was good. Marriage, that is good too. And at the party they pointed to your father. Even though I saw he is old, they let me speak to him, and I could see he is a kind man. That sometimes, when you are older, you have learned enough to be kinder. The young ones, they break so easily, and they can hurt you. Your father, he can never hurt. That is not his way."

We glide into silence a moment. I know what she's saying to me: I am the one who has broken my father, not the other way around. She does not hold it against Abba, all he could not be or do for her: The failing store. His bad back. But me—the young one, the brittle one, the one who can snap like a stalk and hurt others—it's me she holds responsible. This I understand. It's my weight and sadness too. It's as if I'm carrying her youth and mine together. I have no choice. If I fail, I fail her.

"Hey, Ma?"

"Hmm?" Her eyes are kind, but they glimmer with a trace of melancholy.

"I got a job. To help us out."

Her eyes widen. "Where?"

I have to think quickly. "Jamal got it for me. A computer shop. I'm helping out." I can taste the lie on my tongue, metallic, cool.

"What about your summer school?"

"The hours aren't too bad. I can do both."

She looks at me, surprised. Then she sets her hand on my cheek, holds it there just a little longer. Her palm is surprisingly dry and cool. I have to look away so she won't notice the raw catch in my voice, my own wet eyes.

I hand her two fifties and head back into the party, into the night.

CHAPTER 12

THE THING ABOUT BEING A SUPERHERO IS YOU HAVE TO BE OKAY with lying. You're not who you say you are. You're lying for truth. That's the weird thing. You're Iron Man, building a suit of metal, concealing your wounds. Your flaws are your strength. Disguise is your virtue. Just like acting.

With the two hundred left from what Taylor gave me, I register for my English class at LaGuardia. It runs four mornings a week, through the whole summer. To my surprise, I kind of like it. Twenty of us, sitting in a circle and listening to a teacher not much older than me. Messy hair, rumpled plaid shirt over skinny black pants. She doesn't look anything like a teacher. More like a barista at Starbucks. The first day she writes on the whiteboard *English Fundamentals: Intensive Reading & Writing. You Are All Grown-ups. Not Participating Is Not an Option!!*

I'm in such a good mood I decide to get a haircut at the nearby Dominican barber. Already I've worked on my essay. It banged out of me, easy. I've never had words come like that. Rat-a-tat, like one of those plastic guns me and Zahir use at Coney Island. This is *fun*. By the time I'm done, my arms are sore and warm, like I'd been lifting weights.

Instead of the usual flattop, I have the barber do a number two buzz cut. In the mirror I watch my slow disguise, tufts of hair brushing down my ears and neck. A new look: black bristle, like a shadow around my skull, fuzzy-soft to the touch. My new beard growth trimmed.

As I'm twisting out of my chair, I hear, "Hey, man, look at you."

It's Tareq, settling into the next chair.

"Summer cut," I say. Everyone knows about Tareq. *Bagh'a,* they call him—Tiger—with his thick, wavy hair and wide-set eyes. Rumor has it that he was in trouble with the law—something about stolen social security cards. Maybe even worse. Somehow Tareq's lawyer got him off. Last I heard he worked in some kind of auto shop over in Corona.

"And nice threads." He nods to my reflection in the mirror. "Where you been, dressed like that?" He's pointing to my kurta, a cotton blend Amma brought back the last time she went to Bangladesh to visit her family.

I stuff my hands in my pockets, uncomfortable. "Just around." The combs floating in a jar of blue liquid make me queasy. "Gotta go."

He nods. "Don't be a stranger."

Even though he's a pain, I kind of like Tareq. Sure, he's got a bad rep in the community, but whenever he shows up at a party, it gets exciting. Kind of like Ibrahim. Half the stuff he boasts about is bull. But he has imagination. Panache, as Mrs. D would say, one of her favorite words. My parents don't like him, though. *The tiger eats his own tail,* my father says, in that *tsk-tsk* voice of his.

One more stop for the day: Ishrat asked me to help out a charity group. An hour later I find myself in a masjid basement, counting out packages and soup cans, stuffing them into boxes, which are taped and sealed with a little decal that reads *Young Muslims Care.* There are four of us—a serious dude called Mahmoud, who I saw at the conference; Rashid, tattoos twisting up his thick arms, a crocheted skullcap floating on his curls; and Suman, a chubby, placid guy. Then we take ourselves out to eat at a kebab place, digging into plates of skewered meat and watching the soccer game. It's so easy. I tilt in a friendly way, casually ask for phone numbers. Info on a retreat in Pennsylvania. "You should come," Rashid urges me. "The paintball stuff, man. It's seriously down."

After, I'm outside, watching the others angle down the pavement, evening sun shredding across the sky. *What a day,* I think. School, essay done, haircut. My phone is stuffed with names and numbers, even a quick pic of a license as a car drove away. Taylor texted, wants to meet near Roosevelt Avenue. I get the sense he's going to hand me more. The next step.

I'm so elated, my fingers auto-dial Ibrahim—the one

friend who'd be amazed at all I've pulled off. We'd laugh long and hard. I can see him, lean face tipped over, pressing his fist to his mouth, laughing. *Oh, man. That is sick!* he'd say. No one hurt. Just a little spoof.

Then there's a painful commotion stirring in my chest, raw, furious. This isn't a joke. None of it is. I shove the phone back.

Ibrahim. The one person I can't call.

It's a dream, a black-and-white dream, the elevated train shadows slashing down, punctured light wheeling across the windshield in a crazy pattern. I can't tell which part of me is in the dark, which is seen. But I like being here, in this cave of a car, next to Taylor, the upholstery smelling of old hamburgers and dangling air freshener, the creak of his leather jacket, though who knows why he's wearing that in this heat. Even Sanchez in the back, breathing, listening. I'm changing, sliding out of one skin and into a new one, hard, bright, strong. I am metal, and I am what protects and sees. And I'm with someone who gets it. Who knows what I can do.

"This is good," he says when I explain all the numbers I have, the volunteering. Then his words are drowned by the next train, rumbling overhead.

When the air goes still again, I ask, "These groups," I say. "What if they're not doing anything?"

"Then they have nothing to worry about."

"But—"

"Look." He swivels to face me, one hand draped on the wheel. "That's the point. A lot of these organizations, they're really innocent. Not doing anything bad at all. Great stuff, even. But they're a target. You'd be surprised how easy it is for radicals to infiltrate. It's like an infection. Just one, two, and the whole thing spreads."

"But how do I know"—I pause—"who to choose?"

"That's not your job," he replies. His voice is abrupt, hard. I feel the shutting sound, a door, rattling inside me for a long time. It reminds me how Taylor is not just here, with me. There are offices and more offices, growing mazelike behind him. A regular matrix of power—and I'm nothing, just a little bug of information.

Now he turns to me. "You ready for more?"

My heart beats so hard, it's in my throat. Every fiber in me strains. I don't know why, but I want this more than anything. I want to be Taylor, seen and not seen. I want to shift like a lizard in the branches, iridescent, camouflage brown. Every one of my people, the shopkeepers, the old ladies, the hairdressers in the threading salons, they are mine and I am saving them. Somewhere deep inside me is a splinter of doubt, but then it's pushed down, far.

"I—I guess so," I stammer. Why can't I just say yes? "Is there someone in particular I'm following?"

He flashes a cold look at me. "You never ask that, understand?"

I gulp. "Yeah."

"You've got to stay on it. Get serious. We need you to head out to the mosques. Really blend."

"I guess."

I feel his eyes on me, scrutinizing. "If we can work with you, if you keep this up, we're talking a regular salary."

Dazed, I stare out the car window. Another train passes overhead, the pavement showered with confetti strips of light. "How much?"

"About a thousand a month."

A thousand a month. All cash! Once Ibrahim showed me a check stub from when he worked at Chipotle. Twenty hours a week, lettuce threaded in his hair, and after taxes all he had was one hundred thirty-three dollars. *That's why you got to think big,* he always said. Now I feel a burn of satisfaction. *Yo, Ibrahim,* I think, gently rapping my knuckles against the cool window glass. The bristles of my haircut, sharp angles of cheekbones. A slight crook of a smile. *Look where I am, sucker.*

"Hey. Pretty boy. Stop lookin' at yourself."

It's Sanchez, prodding from the backseat. "Don't think it's so easy. You gotta work your butt off. We'll be on you all the time."

My mind's whirring with calculations: three hours in the morning for class. That leaves the rest of the day except for picking up Zahir from the bus, when Amma's busy. A few hours on the weekend at the store.

"You up for this?"

I feel as if my throat is going to explode. "Yes," I whisper. "I can do that."

PART 3

THE DEVOUT

FILE

Masjid Al-Rahman
Address: XXXXX, Brooklyn, NY
Telephone number: XXXXXXXXXX

- CI 1560 reports imam new to congregation. Trained in Saudi Arabia. Prior to affiliation with Masjid Al-Rahman in New York City, traveled to Houston and Pittsburgh. Asserts visiting relatives.
- Initial information and interviews with congregants indicate speakers sympathetic to Muslim conditions overseas invited to speak. No new speakers currently scheduled. No specific instances of retaliatory or hostile actions.

Plan of Action

- Continue pole camera surveillance.
- CI to attend prayer services and monitor imam.
- Continue car license review.
- Continue surveillance of cricket-watching café one block north where many of male congregants gather after prayer.

CHAPTER 13

July blooms hot. Our air conditioner is broken. Ma wedges a fan into our window, but all it does is blow more warm, dirty air into our bedroom. Zahir is whimpering on his mattress, dressed only in boxer shorts, the sheets gummy around his bare legs. The heat gets to him too. Propped against his bed is his sky-blue drawstring backpack—he's in a day camp, and his skin is edged with the tangy smell of chlorine.

I spend most nights doing computer work, keeping up with my Internet watching. I collapse into a universe of cyber identities, avatars, following strands of conversations. My eyes turn owlish, dark. That's when I try to work on my essays for Professor Emily, as I call her. She may look like a barista, but she's one tough teacher. My first essay she gave back slashed with red. *An essay is not a text message,* she wrote. *You know better, Naeem.* I don't know what she means by that. She doesn't know me. No one knows me these days. I don't know myself.

I've changed: I've kept my hair trimmed, my beard shaped into the careful line of a neat goatee like the other devout guys do. I notice when I bound down Seventy-Third Street, the uncles and others, their eyes register differently. I don't get the frown squatting down over their features. Or the blank look of not understanding. I've been slotted into a new place. Good boy. Parents' boy. Working hard, all the time.

The first time I duck into a masjid, it's tough. I feel my wrists shake as I kneel on the carpet. The prayer words slur in my mouth. What do I know? The imam raises his eyes at me, noticing how I keep fumbling to copy everyone else. They aren't stupid. They know guys like me. Informants crawling all over.

Later, as the men gather in the foyer, slipping on shoes and sandals, I try striking up a conversation. Most turn their shoulders, push past me, head out into the white glare of the streets. I leave, discouraged. Nothing to show for my time.

But I go back the next day, and the next. I stay after a special event and help rinse the foil containers and sweep the floor. I play it low-key, steady.

"Where are you from?" the imam asks as I'm leaving. He's young, with a scraggly reddish beard, green eyes almost like Ishrat's. But the skin underneath looks drawn and lined, elephant-gray. As if he doesn't sleep much.

"Brooklyn," I lie.

"Your family name?"

"Hamid."

"I haven't seen you before."

I cock a smile. "Never was too good about the praying stuff. Thought I'd give it a try."

A slight twitching in his cheekbone. Playing it street means I'm a good catch. "Why now?"

I take a breath and then slowly spool out my story. "I was in a dark place," I explain. Then I make my voice go low, hot with shame. "I did a lot of bad things."

He embraces me, his breath scented with pistachio nuts. "Welcome."

Now I go to mosques all the time. As the summer draws down deep and furiously hot, I seek them out. They're a chain of islands across the boroughs: Midwood, Ozone Park, Bay Ridge, Kensington. I follow them, one by one. The small, where you press on a gate, head grazing a brick doorway. The storefront masjids, where they hang strips of thick plastic in the winter, and where all the cabbies go before heading on their routes. The big one, with an imam booming into a microphone, so many men showing up that loudspeakers are fixed to the doors outside so the others can pray in the courtyard. I learn the worn-out shapes of shoes left in cubbies; the chemical smell of a dry cleaner seeping through the walls in one. I bend and fold, touch my forehead to a small rug. The men recite, their melodies twining pure over my head.

After, I sit. I make my features sad and sincere at once. I speak softly, about my black days, my impure thoughts. How I did drugs. Fell off the path. How found, how *seen* I feel now.

It takes time. First their eyes flit with suspicion. No one takes me up. They've been trained not to trust. Then a slow softening. Like Amma, flicking her wrist, slowly working the little balls of dough into supple *paratas*. I'm a boy, after all. A brother. A son. I have to stay with it.

An imam listens, gently gives me Quran passages to read and recite. Or a youth leader takes me aside. There's a film in my head. My eyes do a sweep of the room. Note names, groups, speakers, countries people have visited, if it comes up. Whatever numbers I can get I load into my phone. Friend who I can on Facebook. Sneak-click pictures. Half the stuff I know Taylor doesn't need, but he says it doesn't matter. This is a kind of practice, as good as any devotion.

Ramadan, the month of sunup-to-sundown fasting, will soon be upon us. In the heat, the men will withdraw from their chairs on the pavement, find a cool, dark corner to lay their rug down, adjust it just so, to pray. By four, five o'clock, their eyes are glazed discs. Their heads wobble a little. Everyone listless, limp puddles of waiting. Their carved prayer beads sift through their fingers. Behind the counter I'll hear Amma smacking her dry lips. Her fingers bounce ghostlike on the register. She's faint, but she'll never let on.

And then, just as dark blue darts into the summer sky, Amma will hurry to the back, where she'll make a quick bowl of *moori*, swirling the bits of chopped green chilis in puffed rice. Then I'll hear the snap of the microwave door, the pan sliding inside. Tendrils of spice and oily meat smell drift out. My own stomach rumbles in expectation, scraped dry; I'm gasping with hunger.

"You are fasting this year?" Abba asks me. His eyebrows, bushy, unkempt, are raised.

I grin. "Yeah, why not?"

This has been a sore subject between us forever. I never really fasted. Like everything I tried, I did it and didn't do it. It was like my going to the mosque in the old days. Or my Saturday religious school, most of which passed through me. *You have no staying power!* Abba would complain.

"Hey, Abba," I say. "What do you say we go on Friday to the big mosque?" This is where we used to go for the major holidays, even though it's in another neighborhood.

He casts me a suspicious glance. "Why do you want to go there?"

I shrug. "For a change. It's been a long time."

He shakes his head, turns back to swabbing down the counter. Why does he use the same shredded gray rag? There's an explosion detonating hard against my chest. The shabbiness of everything infuriates me. All that money I can make. More contacts, more work; I just have to keep going. That will wipe it all away, the shame of Amma squeezing every last drop of detergent from the bottle, or scraping the last of the mutton curry out of the microwave container. I hate that her grocery cart is broken and she drags it on the pavement with its dented wheel. I feel my dollar bills twinkle in my pocket. I will buy it all for them: the new TV, the shopping cart, as many comic books as Zahir wants. I will be like that guy blowing on his Starbucks coffee, nice scarf cowled around his neck. A car, so we can drive to Rockaway Beach and feel the briny wavelets slap against our ankles.

I calm down. I see Abba has joined the men who pray in the alleyway, right by the small masjid. He signals to me with his eyes. I chuck off my shoes, kneel down beside him. I can feel his heat and breathe his father-smell, pungent, angry, familiar.

Forgive me, I silently mouth as I bend too, my heart sore.

Later, as I'm turning the corner, I see Mrs. Khan, hands on her hips, talking to a cop. Mrs. Khan is always complaining about how hard it is, competing with the big places on the corner. She keeps a hawk eye on their prices, cuts her costs by hiring only one or two Mexicans and a girl who works the cash register.

A policeman is arguing with her about setting out her bags of garbage too soon. "I cannot help it. My husband, he is resting inside. Heart brings trouble. Heat. I have no helpers to put out."

"Not now, ma'am. It's blocking the pedestrians. You should know better." He adds, "This isn't news to you."

"I know. But with Ramadan and husband not well—"

"Ma'am." He rests his fingers on his thick belt. His voice has turned stern, impatient. "Don't make me issue you a summons."

I take a shaky step forward, stand next to Mrs. Khan. I make sure to let my hands hang by my pockets. "Don't worry, Auntie. I'll take care of it."

She turns to me, grateful. She's sweating something awful; there's a furry mustache of sweat over her lip. "I didn't see you there, Naeem."

"What time should I come back?"

"Evening time. Six, seven o'clock." She makes a helpless gesture. "Two boys called in sick today. And we got big shipment. Many boxes."

I turn to the cop. For the first time, I don't flinch. I stand, full on, shoulders spread in my shirt seams. My gaze meets his visored eyes. *I'm one of you,* I think. "I've got it, sir," I say to him. "I'll make sure it's done right."

By nighttime word has gotten back to my parents of the good I've done in the neighborhood. After Mrs. Khan I stopped off and helped one of the old guys fold up his table and put away his wares. For once I'm the kid with the golden heart, doing my duty. "You should have heard Mrs. Khan going on about you! 'What a sweet boy, what a generous boy!'" Even my father, sunk in his La-Z-Boy

133

chair, grunts with approval. "See, Abba," I say. "I'm not a lost cause."

"Lost cause," he mutters, rattling his newspaper. But I can hear just a little pleasure in his voice.

The next evening, when we break the fast, it's different between us. Amma has a surprise. "We are going to eat up there."

"Where?" Zahir asks, puzzled.

She giggles, pushing back a moist strand of hair. "Just follow."

Nights back in Dhaka we would sometimes go up to our rooftop. We'd duck under the strung laundry, sit on woven mats, listening to the rapid *beep-beep* of traffic that never stops. It's the same tonight. The elevator is broken, so me and Abba and Zahir sneak up the stairs, warm bowls tucked against our stomachs. Amma is carrying the heaviest pot and refuses to let anyone help.

On the top floor Mrs. Persaud, the Guyanese lady, cracks open her door and scowls. She's always complaining that we make too much noise or are stealing her mail, so we ignore her.

"Do you want to join?" Amma calls out. We're supposed to always break the fast with company, so Amma is trying her best to include Mrs. Persaud. Before she shuts the door, I see just a quiver of a smile.

Then we're scuffing across the tar roof. Just over the concrete edge we can see the slender spires of Manhattan. The Brooklyn-Queens Expressway rushes in the distance, constant as a river. Otherwise the streets lie quiet around us. We sit right there, on a cotton spread. First Amma pops open a plastic container and hands out dates. We each slide one into our parched mouths, bite into the sugary pulp, so sweet our teeth ache.

She pulls the top off her big pot and reveals what she's cooked: crabs swimming in sauce—how did she find them? Amma always used to tell how when she was a little girl, the servant would return to her village and bring a whole bag of the black-and-pink-shelled creatures, spilling them onto newspaper on the kitchen floor. She had loved them, the sweet taste of the meat that comes only from Bengal waters, elbowing and fighting her sisters to see who could suck more flesh from the spiny legs. We do the same, me and Zahir, our mouths smeared. Abba looks on approvingly.

I can see Amma, the flyaway wisps at her temple when she leans over the counter, using the heel of her hands to smash garlic or scrape knobs of ginger on the *bondi* blade the way her mother's servants did, on the floor. But here Amma does it all. Immigrating has a way of turning everything upside down: who's on top, who's on the bottom. The Aslam brothers thought to put their livery-car money together and bought a shop on a scruffy stretch of Hillside Avenue. Now you have to double- and triple-park to get inside. Who knew?

That's what Ibrahim once showed me: how to tip the glass of possibility the other way. We were partners. Every day he had a new idea: Open our own club. Invent a new app.

Not anymore, I think sadly.

"You never talk about your class, Naeem," Amma says, interrupting my thoughts.

"It's going well," I tell her.

"Well well or just well?"

I laugh. "Well well." I add, "I like the teacher. She's cool."

"Naeem is on the computer all the time," Zahir pipes in.

"Is that right?"

I start. "Um, yeah. Research for my class." I glance over at my little brother. He lifts his face to me, eyes shining. My nerves go taut. Has he been watching me?

"So what do you say, Abba?" I ask, thinking about the three days of celebrating the end of Ramadan. "For Eid Ul-Fitr? Why don't we go to the big mosque?"

He laughs. "You are persistent, Naeem. This I haven't seen before."

I feel a hard, angry heat, not sure whether to be pleased or upset.

"Something goes wrong, you give up."

"Not anymore."

"No," he admits. "Not so much." He sucks on one of the crab legs and tosses the shell down onto a plate. I think about how few times I see us like this, relaxing.

"What about a day off, Abba?" I ask. "At the beach? We haven't gone to Rockaway in ages."

We used to pack up a cooler and take a bus down Wood-haven Boulevard. It was a long ride, but we didn't care. Once there, Amma rolled up the bottoms of her pants, the little waves washing against her calves. Abba walked the length of the sand. The wind seemed to rub his face young. We felt it then: ocean, horizon, stretching in every direction possible.

"Rockaway!" Zahir calls out. "Yes!"

Abba's eyes gleam in the dark as he considers. "Your mother and I. We have so much work." But I can hear his voice softening. "Let us see."

The change, it's ringing deep around me. A deep, brassy sound. A shine of approval. I hear and see it on the streets now. Naeem, who gave his parents so much trouble once, now turned obedient son. I am more than they can see. Even with the fasting I've never felt so light. I am a nighthawk, winging from neighborhood to neighborhood, snatching up secrets, keeping them safe.

I take the train to Thirtieth Avenue, zigzagging past the houses with their tiny front gardens and flourishing pots of sunflowers. It's easy by the Bengali areas. Not much to pick up on. Mostly the old guys who hang outside after prayers—the younger ones have cabs to drive, jobs to get to. No story there. I go over to Little Egypt in Astoria, hookah lounges behind dimmed glass. After a while I realize they're all talking Arabic and French—what good am I listening to them? Stupid police. As if we're all the same.

Still I walk and walk, just because I like it, hopping on and off at different stops, following the branching spine of subways. My legs are tired. I come home and sleep harder than I ever have. The work suits me. Being paid to wander. Now, that's a good deal.

The only problem is there's nothing to report. Nothing.

Friday night in Kensington I hang by a little triangle park near the shops. The mothers lug their bulging shopping bags, exhausted from fasting and now getting ready to cook, their younger kids licking Mr. Softee ice cream. The men sit and chat. Gossip lingers in the evening air: who's got a bad back, who reneged on a loan and is in trouble. Whose daughter is getting married to a boy they don't like. They give me that smile-frown of an elder. And then they gather themselves and walk slowly back to the masjid, kurtas fluttering like pennants in the evening's ruddy light.

Nothing here, I text Taylor.

Join the study group.

Roger that.

When I meet up with Taylor, he slips me a wad: five hundred dollars. That's the most I've gotten so far, though I feel a little dip of disappointment. "I thought you said a thousand. . . ."

Sanchez grins. "You haven't gotten us much. Thought you were in the know. In on the community."

I puff out my chest. "I am."

"Show us the money and we give you more money." He rubs his fingers together, kisses the tips.

Angry, I stuff what they gave me into my pocket. No way I'm going to let this Sanchez guy cut me down. He's trying to drive a wedge between me and Taylor. Make it seem like I'm not worth much.

As if reading my mind, Taylor smiles.

"It's only been a few weeks, man. Keep at it."

Back home, I peel off the bills, save fifty for me, and give the rest to Abba. His eyes go wide. Amma lets out a small cry. "Buy the stock you need," I say.

"What should we get?" Abba asks Amma.

"Stationery," I answer.

They both turn to me, surprised.

"That's what you need. Envelopes. Paper. Post-its. Good pens. Not that junk you have. There isn't a Staples nearby. Everybody hates going there anyway. And school stuff. You know how it is. Some science project and you don't have colored paper. They just want to pick it up on their way home."

"Maybe we can get some new displays!" Amma suggests, excited.

Abba shakes his head. "This money you gave us. That won't be enough."

She takes the bills from him, tucks them into her pocket. "You wait."

The next day, Amma goes right to the Bangladeshi bank and sees about securing a small line of credit for new stock. It's as if the part of her mind that was always worrying about me has freed up. Later my parents sit at the dinette table, heads together, flipping through an office supplies catalog. Carefully, they fold down pages, circle what they want. This goes on all night; I can hear them whispering on the other side of the thin wall, scheming.

"No, no," Amma says. "We need investment. Copier machine. I've heard the lease is not so expensive."

"Maybe," Abba assents. I've never heard them this way: talking, planning, as if there really is a future here.

By the end of the week, I'm in such a good mood I meet Zahir at his bus stop. He comes bounding off the steps, nylon bag hiked over his shoulder, surprised. His face brightens. These days, with all my work, dashing here and there, it's rare I pick him up.

"You wanna come with me?" I ask.

"Yes, yes!" Then he pauses. "But where?"

"For an ice cream."

He nods vigorously. Sometimes I feel such a pang, seeing Zahir. He's not like me. Or at least, not like what I was at his age. He's pure and frisky-bright. I worry what will happen when he goes to middle school. They'll eat him whole, the tough kids. I started talking to Abba and Amma about paying for tutoring for him so he can test into the magnet schools. But either they're afraid to let him out of the neighborhood or there just isn't enough money for extra help.

We sit at the ice cream parlor, the old-fashioned vinyl booths behind us, stools spinning beneath our legs. My stomach's scraped dry, but I just watch him spoon up his hot-fudge sundae. It pleases me, to give him this much.

"So I got something for you."

"What?"

"Can't say. Unless you promise me something."

His face wrinkles into a puzzled expression. He looks like a little gnome, crescent-shaped indents around his eyes from his swim goggles. Out of my backpack, I slide a book I found. *Middle-School Math*.

"But I'm not in middle school," he says, disappointed.

"I know. But you should get started."

I see his thin shoulders slump. This is definitely not what he had in mind.

"Here's the thing," I explain. "You promise to do two pages of this every night and I'll give you this."

I pull from my pack a huge stack of Marvel comics. Twenty of them, to be exact. The New Avengers. I bought them in a zine store I found one day, deep in Brooklyn. Zahir gives such a whoop, legs kicking out from under him, I'm sure he's going to fall off the stool.

"All of these are mine?" He's so excited, his voice is squeaky-high.

"All of them," I say quietly. "If you do your math, Zahir."

"You bet!"

"Our secret, okay? That way you can surprise Amma and Abba. Get yourself ahead in school."

He nods vigorously. When we stroll back to the store, I let him carry all the comic books, and he stops every few feet to look at them. His eyes shine with disbelief. Suddenly, he turns, flings his arms around my waist, and buries his head in my stomach. "Thank you, Naeem," he whispers.

CHAPTER 14

"Anything new?"

"Not much."

"I noticed."

My stomach hurts. For the first time, instead of a quick meeting where they hand me a few bills, Taylor and Sanchez and me are meeting in the open. Totally not procedure. They've driven me to some neighborhood in a part of Queens I don't know, which has me on edge. It's like I've been brought into the station house all over again. Or hauled up before Mrs. D or one of my old teachers for a missed assignment. I haven't delivered.

"Though you look good."

"Thanks."

"Filled out. Confident. What're you eating these days?"

"Not a whole lot." I scratch at my jaw, which is itchy from the new beard growth. "I'm fasting."

His eyebrows rise. "You're really into this. Playing the role."

"It's not a role," I say, annoyed.

I notice Taylor has on sunglasses and a jacket, even though it's warm out. Sanchez trudges behind. We pass houses with aluminum siding, tight up next to each other. One's got four mailboxes, a thick rope of cables snaking up the side of the house, four satellite dishes tilted on the roof. I know these places—where the Dominican or the Chinese busboys live on mattresses, sometimes taking shifts. They keep their money in nylon pouches tight against their bodies. Abba once lived like that, when he first came here. To this day he always sleeps in a few minutes after my stepmother rises, says he wants to know what it feels to stretch his toes in his own bed.

Taylor stops in front of an arbor dripping with plump bunches of glistening grapes. He plucks one and pops it in his mouth. "Want one?" he asks.

I hesitate.

"Sorry. I forgot."

Just a grape, I tell myself. I take it, and the juice squirts tart into my mouth; the seeds crunch. I almost want to cry out with pleasure. Then I'm flooded with shame. Who am I? A guy who's faking he's devout? Or is this me?

"Not bad, huh? My grandmother used to have grapes out back at our house," he says.

"Where was that?"

"Bellerose. Right by Alley Pond Park." He grabs another grape. "She had a fig tree too. Brought it all the way from Italy, crazy lady. Every fall she'd cover it with burlap. I swear she treated it like another baby."

"So your family is from Italy?" I ask. "How'd you get a name like Taylor?"

He shrugs. "Believe it or not, my grandfather was a tailor. Sort of. He cut patterns for a company. My parents thought Taylor sounded right. Gave the old man his due. He died before I was born. But the old lady, she lived in a bedroom off the kitchen. My whole life."

"But you don't—you don't look Italian," I protest.

He smiles. "They're from the north, that's all. Blond."

"There're all kinds," Sanchez laughs, from behind.

All kinds, I think, rolling the phrase in my mind. I've always pegged Taylor as some all-American Fordham guy. But it's as if I can see his house, a wedge of brick and Tudor, the little bedroom, even the arbor draped in purple grapes out back. Grand Central Parkway humming past like a river. His family is from somewhere else too.

But what's going on here? The three of us, walking out in the open, sunlight on our heads, talking about growing up in Bellerose. We're not supposed to be seen together. That much I know.

"So," he says. "Nothing turn up?"

"I told you. It's just prayers. Gossip."

"You have a problem with this work?" Sanchez asks. " 'Cause we're kinda wonderin'. We paid you."

"Not much."

"You didn't give us much." He adds, "We're not paying you to make friends. Find someone to invite to your wedding."

"Very funny."

I wish Sanchez weren't on my back, breathing fire. The guy is intense. Like he's going to break into a street fight any second. If I could just be alone with Taylor. Sometimes I can feel a connection, invisible, hard to catch, between us. It's all in his shoulders and his walk, the way he cups his keys, cuts me a smile. It was there that first evening, with him and Sanchez. He's signaling me a way out. So different from Abba, who wants me to duck my head as he does, fold myself and pray. Stay unseen. No trouble. Heart still as a hibernating animal.

Taylor turns to me. There's a crease of worry in his brow. "Seriously, Naeem. You have questions?"

I pause, then working up my nerve, ask, "Do you ever feel weird about doing this? Snitching on people you might know?"

His jaw tenses. "The thing about being a cop is you're a skeptic. Even about your best friend, your neighbor."

"That's hard."

"Is it? No one ever tells the whole truth, Naeem."

I give a little shiver. Is he talking about me?

"Even you," he says, as if reading my mind.

He clicks open the car and we all get in, me in the front with Taylor. Pulling out an iPad, he swipes the screen and then hands it to me. "You ever see one of these?"

It's a recruiting video. The screen is black. Then soft voices, lapping water, strands of soothing music. A call to prayer stirs some deep and old place inside me. Soft focus on a guy about my age sitting cross-legged on the ground, a semiautomatic set casually on his knees. I see his mouth moving around familiar words. The words are all good: *God. Truth. Purpose.*

But I can see a cruel glow beneath his skin.

It's his eyes. Like stars that have gone dead.

"That's some messed-up stuff," Sanchez says, low.

I nod. My mouth is coated dry, as it always is this time of day, from the fasting. The forbidden tang of grape on my tongue.

"You know how many hits this video got before we took it down?"

I shake my head. A queasiness washes up behind my ribs. "What do you want me to do?"

"It's the offshoots we're keeping an eye on."

"Conversations on the side," Sanchez puts in.

"Lone wolves."

"There's some activity?" I ask.

He shakes his head. "You know we can't tell you that. It's bad enough we talk to you this much."

"These guys are for real," Sanchez puts in. "No joke. This is war. We need foot soldiers who got discipline. 'Cause sometimes, with you, I'm not feeling it."

I don't say anything.

"No free rides here," Sanchez says. "Haul in some bet-

146

ter intel. Good tips mean money. You gotta work for this, baby."

"You got it?" Taylor asks.

I stare out the window, watch an old Chinese woman sweep her pavement, back and forth, sending up little puffs of gray dirt. So that's what this is all about. It's about protecting people like my family, my neighbors, just trying to make it, to keep our hold here. All of us pressed up against each other, working so hard: the remittances wired to family back home, the weekly calls on the phone card, the nylon bags stuffed with clothes and hair dryers and lotions, zippers bursting, dragged across the floor at JFK airport.

They are the tattoo on my heart; they are my electric circuits, lighting up my veins. They are my Gotham. I can feel every one of us, squeezed into the little stores and houses, aluminum siding falling off. Every one of us yearning. You can feel that rush to the subway every morning, the sky pink and brand-new, the trains sucking their doors open and closed, scooping us in. We snake and move toward the city. It trembles through every one of us, the ambition, the striving, the want. And I must save them.

"Got it," I breathe.

CHAPTER 15

MAYBE I NEEDED THAT. A PEP TALK. REALIGNMENT. REMEMBERing those sick dudes on the video. Nausea at the back of my throat. School too: I got a C on my last essay for Professor Emily. *Is there a thesis statement here?* she wrote. *And what about punctuation?* Time to double down. Focus. A few more weeks, another payment, and I can register for math in the fall. When I show up at Taslima's office the day after my meeting with Taylor and Sanchez, she tells me, "I've decided to promote you."

"Me?" I drop my canvas bag in the corner and start twisting open a bottle of juice. It's murderous hot out there, and the bus was fifteen minutes late. I notice Ishrat is also in the office today, sitting at the corner of the desk stapling stacks of colored paper.

"Don't look so shocked," Taslima remarks. "Ishrat is impressed with you. Go figure."

"Maybe it's my hair," I joke.

"Yeah. Right." She reaches over and affectionately rubs my scalp. "What hair these days? Seriously. We're supposed to run some youth leadership programs with the mosque this summer. Ishrat thinks you can connect with the kids. You can be a liaison. She's your female equivalent."

"Hardly," Ishrat laughs. She presses the heel of her hand on the stapler and it makes a loud chewing noise.

I feel a little heat under my skin. Ishrat's exactly the sort of girl I usually avoid, the type who would tease me and my friends from across the cafeteria table, but then if you gave it back to her, she'd back away, shy. But here we're shoulder to shoulder, getting bruises on our palms from too much stapling. Too close.

Most of the kids who come streaming through the doors don't seem to know where to go—they look like cows in a pen, aimlessly bumping into each other, shoving chips in their mouths. I know Taslima and Ishrat have been showing up at every youth and student group and high school and mosque, pulling the kids in. Ishrat is busy making little baskets for the older kids who are fasting, or at least trying it out. She's festooned them with ribbons and small prayer cards and tucked in snacks inside tissue.

A slender girl steps into the room and looks around uncertainly. She's thin, looks about fifteen, and is skittish, as if she's not sure she wants to be here. "Hey, Noor!" Ishrat does a big arm-rolling motion. "You came!"

The girl gives a shaky nod.

Up close I can see Noor is a funny mix: tight jeans with zippers at the ankles, a peach-colored scarf that matches her nails, which are tipped in shiny decals. A fluorescent string knapsack hangs from her thin shoulders, saggy with books. She keeps her arms pressed across her chest.

"It'll be fun! You'll see. We've got activities and group talk and guest speakers." She thrusts out a marker. "You want to write good wishes on the cards?"

Poor Ishrat—she reminds me of my stepmother, with her round face, working so earnestly at everything. I want to reach out, wipe off the sweat that's showing on her upper lip, and say *Don't try so hard.*

Noor looks dubious. "That's okay. I'll just watch."

She shifts awkwardly to sit on a folding chair in a corner and takes a book out of her little knapsack. The others who have taken their registration folders are whooping it up, girls flirting; one boy's sitting on a table, sneaker laces tied together, annoyed at the girl who did it to him. Noor ignores them all, lost in her book.

"Her parents weren't sure they wanted to send her," Ishrat explains. "We should keep an eye on her."

All that week, I'm at it with new zeal, fastening myself to a schedule. Wanting to prove Sanchez wrong, find them something solid. First my morning English class, and then I head over to Taslima's youth leadership camp, which she's running through mid-August. Mostly it's a hodgepodge of feel-good conversations about identity and politics and community service. The kids are all over Queens, scrubbing clean an old mural on the wall of a bank, forking up litter in Forest Park, or sometimes speakers come and give talks.

In the afternoon we break and sit under the waving trees, where Ishrat, who's majoring in social work, leads us in "group," discussions about getting to know ourselves. At first everyone is shy or the boys can't stop making it a joke, tossing pretzels at each other. Then they settle down and the stories slowly leak out: The people on the bus who stare at your mother because she's wearing a hijab. The kid who changed his name from Mohammed to Mo. The others who are paying attention to those creeps online. Turning on the news to find out about some Bangladeshi store clerk pummeled by a customer. The confusion, the anger. It seeps in all the time, like rust. No wonder they twist on the grass; no wonder they flash with annoyance when Ishrat presses them.

I treat group like acting. I know how to idle on the side, start up a new line of talk. A casual remark about all the wars in Muslim countries. Poor orphans. I look for that click of light in their eyes. A struck match. How much anger is burning? It's almost too easy, especially with the younger ones.

"You hear about that drone attack? Is that why our parents came here? To pay for that?"

A boy named Ashraf sits up. "Why is it whenever there is a terrorist attack, we have to explain ourselves?"

"Yeah, why do they assume there's a connection?" a girl throws in.

"It's true, there isn't a connection," Ishrat replies, calm. "But we are new to this country. So people are suspicious."

"That's profiling. That's Islamophobia!"

The others stir, upset. Ishrat doesn't budge. "Maybe it is. But what is your job? Is it to hunker down and be furious? Or to explain yourself? Every outsider, every immigrant has had to do this."

Ashraf stares sulkily at the floor. "I didn't sign up for that job."

I drop a few more provocative comments, but they don't go anywhere. Ishrat always firmly leads us back to a quieter place. When we break, she draws me aside. "No more of that talk," she tells me. I see another side of her: the tough girl who doesn't take any bull from anyone. "Taslima says she knows you. You're family. So I'll cut you some slack. But nobody believes that kind of stuff, okay?"

"Yeah. Sure." I press the shakiness out of my voice.

When no one is looking, I slip away and send a stream of texts. Names, if I can get them. Guest lecturers. How many times the kids pray, if they do at all. But I sense an impatience on the other end, dissatisfaction. *That all?*

Yes.

Keep at it.

At the end of the day, I drive back with Taslima, Ishrat drowsing in the front seat, her head propped against the rattling window. Strands of her hair, which have escaped from her scarf, lie damp against her neck. She looks exhausted. She gives everything to these kids—and more. It makes me want to brush her hair aside, words welling in my throat, all I'd like to tell her.

When we pull up to Ishrat's house, I see it's much nicer than I imagined: a brick Tudor, a beige Audi parked in the driveway. Geraniums sprout in little pots on the brick stoop. Carved metal gates that are popular with a lot of the *desi* families, showing how far they've come.

As we're opening the trunk to unload some of Ishrat's supplies, a voice calls out, "You girls want some help?"

We both turn. Dusk is falling, a low, slanted light scattering off the stoops and fire escapes, making it hard to see. Then the figure draws near and we can pick out a familiar, shambling walk, thick shoulders. Tareq.

Taslima stiffens. "That's okay."

"Come on, Tas!"

"Really. I got it." She reaches down into the open trunk, angry, stiff. "Thanks anyway. Naeem's here to help."

He swivels, gives me the once-over. "Naeem, man! Didn't see you there! How are you? You working for her?" There's a curl of surprise in his voice. "She give you a hard time?"

"She's okay."

"Yeah, well, don't let her put you down."

The trunk slams shut. "You done, Tareq?" Taslima's

153

voice is taut, bouncing with annoyance. "Some of us have work to do."

He does a fake clutch to his chest. "Ooh, Tas. You always break my heart." Then, looking at me, he jabs a finger at Ishrat. "That your girl?"

Ishrat, who has been staying quiet, shifts away, embarrassed. Our hips nearly bump.

"Just kidding, man. I know you're still working the field." He peers close. "That's not a beard I see?"

A little warmth creeps up my nape. "Yes."

"What do you know," he murmurs. I can't tell if he's hostile or laughing behind those crinkly eyes.

Taslima shouldn't get so riled up, I think as I lug a box to Ishrat's house. He's just a peacock. A big mouth. Not so different from Ibrahim. Where is he now? I wonder. At his parents' apartment? I can't place him in my mind these days. Not without him texting, urging me to do some nutty thing. When I turn back to the street, Tareq seems to have vanished into the grainy early evening. I feel a brush of sadness, I don't know why.

That Friday we herd the kids into the city for a boat cruise. They're hyperexcited, the boys nudging and elbowing each other on line. I notice a few people, tourists mostly, slide their eyes over us, especially the girls' head scarves fluttering in the wind. When it's time to show bags, the security man really checks the boys' backpacks, unzips every compartment.

154

Then comes Noor, lugging her huge vinyl bag filled with Japanese anime books. She still doesn't socialize much with the other kids. Prefers her books. Or spends a lot of time staring at her nails—every day she's got a different polish—black, purple, glittery decals.

"Hold on there," he says.

She trembles a little, fingers clutched around her straps. She looks so pale.

"Open it. All the way."

She turns it over, so her makeup case and lip gloss jars and books go scattering to the floor. Embarrassed, she scoops them up. Am I wrong? Is the guard extra irritated with her? Or am I imagining it? That's the thing that spins your head. You never know. I suddenly feel protective of her, of all these kids, seeing how exposed they are. Confusion rolls through me. Isn't that what I'm doing—tracking them? Am I so different from that guard?

Once the boat glides away from the pier, the kids go nuts—rushing in different directions on the swaying deck, pointing at the sights, swiveling the viewers on their holders. The Hudson River glitters like foil in the sun. The skyline eases past. It's one of those corny New York things that no one ever does. And it's beautiful.

Then I spot Noor standing off to the side. She's not with the other kids. She's leaning her elbows on the railing, her face tilted toward the sun, her big bag wedged between her ankles. It's only when I get close that I notice her face is wet with tears.

"Hey," I say softly. I make sure not to stand too close to her. "You okay?"

She remains still. I notice how slender her shoulders are; her features are very fine, as if drawn with a thin, light brown pencil.

"Noor? What's the matter?"

When she turns to me, strangely enough, she's smiling. "I'm just so happy. I've never done this." She takes a breath. "I've never been on a subway. None of this."

"That's great."

Tears start sliding down her cheeks. "I just want to be normal," she whispers. "I want to go to camp and Coney Island and . . ." She uses her sleeve to wipe her eyes and doesn't finish.

"Hey, you are normal," I say.

"Yeah, right."

"Why don't you go hang with the other kids? Don't let them monopolize all the good viewers."

"They're not my friends, really." Then she does a small, timid move toward me. "Can I tell you something?"

"Sure."

"I have a boyfriend."

I grow alert. "That right?"

"Yeah." She looks very pleased.

"Here?" I nod toward a clump of our boys who are fighting over a bag of chips.

"Oh, no!" She puts her hand over her mouth. "I met him . . . online. On a website."

"What do you guys talk about?"

"He's very nice. He sends me books. About faith. And he tells me so many nice things. He's not like these boys." Her brow furrows. "So immature!"

"They're not so bad," I offer. "They'll grow up."

"But he is grown up already." Her voice has turned a little cool, which annoys me. This private life, this connection, makes her feel superior, different from the goofballs scrambling on the deck around us.

"Is that okay? Having a boyfriend? I mean, you're not supposed to do that, right?" She lowers her eyes, blushing. "He is very serious about us. And he is teaching me a lot. Did you know there are places? Where you can go and live a good life. Where you can be useful."

"Your boyfriend tell you about that?"

"Yes," she whispers. "He is there now."

I try to keep my voice casual. "So what's the website where you met?"

But Noor's face has gone blank. She's withdrawn. "I—I should go," she stammers, and snatches up her bag. My stomach twists, watching her slip away, her small hand leaning on the rail to keep her balance.

After that, I can't stop thinking about Noor; she's a burr that's latched on to my thoughts. Tell someone, I think. But who? She doesn't show for camp the morning after the boat ride. Or the next.

"I'll call her mom," Ishrat assures me. But all she can do is leave a message. "Maybe after Eid," she says.

But I wonder. I know how it works. During the day kids like her are good. They say the right words or help their mothers clear the table. But when the bedroom door clicks shut, they switch on computers. Their fingers click. A magic door whooshes open. They are someone else. They wear armor, smudge their eyes with kohl, wield swords. They are invincible. I know because I am different too. I walk the streets, peer through the fire escapes into windows, try to imagine these shining avatars, insects flicking and burning through night screens.

The last days of Ramadan dwindle down. The days of forgiveness, they're called. The neighborhood is turning loud and blaring and gaudy. Everywhere is the frantic air of shopping. On one corner, people surround a table piled high with packages of new bedsheets. The old guys' tables are mounded with new skullcaps and beads. Women rush past, carrying flat plastic bags with new saris.

Taslima and a few of the girls from the camp are setting up a henna table to raise money, joining the other make-shift stands that now line Seventy-Fourth Street. Each table has laminated pages of designs, women selling their handi-work for ten, twenty dollars. They'll be there all evening, even as their stomachs gnaw with hunger; even as others go home to break the fast, they'll keep squirting tubes of gelled henna on the backs of women's hands.

I'm inside a sari store where shoppers stand shoulder to shoulder at the counter, bargaining in sharp, happy voices.

The other day a sari for Amma caught my eye—cream with an emerald-green band. But I've only got a twenty in my pocket. I hit auto-dial for Taylor.

"Hey."

"Hey."

There's a pause. "Long time no hear. You got anything?"

"Not much." I want to add, *It's Eid. Give me a little bonus.* Fat chance.

Quiet on the other end. Not friendly quiet either. "Look. Sanchez and I have been talking. This youth stuff you're doing. I think you gotta give it a rest."

"You haven't paid me in a while."

"You haven't given me anything. Move on."

I knew it would come to this. I've dropped down on the number of mosques I visit. Missed a prayer group I was supposed to track. And I haven't checked out any other campus groups. But the kids are growing on me. I kind of like hanging with them. Ishrat wants me to lead an acting class. I have to remember it isn't my job. Not really.

In the background, I can hear Sanchez. "He's a punk. He doesn't have anything. Cut him loose, man."

I feel a surge of anger. It's that tank of a Sanchez again, swiveling away, as if I'm not worth it.

"You there, Naeem?"

I could give Noor's name. Isn't that why I called? Tell about her flirtations online. How she hasn't come back. It's nothing. Just a name. Do it. Shut that Sanchez guy up already. Taylor will give me another few hundred, for sure.

159

But then I remember Noor leaning over the rail, the breeze blowing back her scarf. *I just want to be normal.*

"Naeem? You got something?" Taylor asks.

"Soon." I hang up before I give him anything more.

Across the street, I catch sight of Taslima and her girls, and head over.

"Hey, Tas—"

She turns. "Yeah?"

"Do me a favor. After Eid, can you follow up on Noor?"

She gives me a puzzled look. "What's up?"

"I dunno. Just a little worried about her, that's all. She goes online a lot—"

There's a flash of alarm in Taslima's face as she registers this. I don't have to say anything more. She pats me on the arm. "You're a good kid," she whispers. Then she thrusts up her sleeve, showing the scroll-like pattern down her wrist. "Wanna stay?"

"Nah, thanks."

But I can't keep my eyes off the girls, who are laughing, comparing designs. Even Taslima, with her worries, her severe little mouth, the slash of her hair, looks happy, relaxed. Next to me, a father tries a new skullcap on his son, pats it approvingly. I love this. All of us getting to be out in the open, not afraid. Not hidden at all. When we can be ourselves.

Then I step back into the crowds and a seam of forgiveness folds over and around me.

160

CHAPTER 16

FOR EID UL-FITR WE LOAD INTO A BORROWED CAR, THE FIRST time in ages, and drive over to the big mosque. Zahir in the back with me, his skinny arms goose-bumped from the air-conditioning. I'm feeling good, tight in here with the family.

What I love about this holiday has nothing to do with belief or Islam. It's about quiet. Three days stretch before us. First we'll go to prayers and then we have visits and eating and more visits. Maybe a trip to the mall or, if Abba is in the mood, an amusement park for Zahir—and me too.

This morning when we go for prayers, it's about submitting to that still space inside. My best times with Abba are when we walk, he with his wrists at the small of his back. We don't say a word. A tether between us. Sometimes our shoulders bump. That's all. That's as good as any prayer.

"This year we will have more luck," Amma says. "I am

161

hopeful." She spreads her fingers through her hair, which has been clipped back with studded combs. They match her little turquoise purse, her outfit, which she bought on Eid special with the extra money I gave her.

As we're nearing the masjid, we see a barricade across the street; a cop waves us toward a side street. Other barricades are placed at the far end. "So many police," my mother murmurs.

"It's for our own good," Abba replies.

But I see the hesitation in his face, how his shoulders pull back as we walk toward the open area. Amma, though, is lighthearted; she angles toward the women's side, which is roped off with a string of plastic flags. I can still hear her voice singing high, like a little girl's, while we make our way to the big lawn, where the prayers are being held.

Zahir skips beside us, chin tipped up, eager. He knows that there's a big meal and sweets later, and a gift, pulled out from under Abba and Amma's bed.

Abba's movements are stiff and nervous. I see how hard it is for him to even come here, to show his face openly at Eid prayers, after so long. We find a place on one of the long white cloths that have been spread out on the ground. There must be hundreds of people sitting cross-legged before the makeshift stage. We arrive in time to stand and say our *niyat,* our intention. And then I am with the others, hands up by my ears, across my chest, reciting the *Surah Al-Fatiha,* then another *Surah.* We bend and kneel. I touch my forehead to the ground. When I sit back on my haunches, I feel as if I'm floating, not fully here. What do I see and hear? The rustle of feet as we hear the call, move and bend again in unison. Men all around me: some hunched and fervent, others distracted. Boys wandering between legs. A baby wails. Two kids are smacking each other with balloons. My mind drifts. I try letting the prayers pour down, flow over and around me.

The prayers are rising, louder, more insistent. More men squeeze in next to us. Our thighs bang. I shut my eyes, let myself duck inside, like the old days.

And then I'm coming back for air: everyone standing up, the men shaking out their loose pants, embracing one another. Abba, who is busy talking with some friends, turns to me and says, "Go find your mother. It will take a long time with all the cars."

I head across the lawn and scan for Amma in the women's area. Under a canopy of trees, I catch sight of Ishrat, who is watching two girls chasing each other on the grass. She gives me a shy smile; her eyes shine under the dark leaves.

"Asalamu alaikum," I greet her, moving near.

"Alaikum asalam." She's all dressed up in a blue shalwar kamize, matching eye shadow on her lids. We sway there a few minutes, embarrassed, several feet between us. I can't stay here too long, the two of us unaccompanied. Usually when we're at the camp, we can use the excuse of gossiping about the kids, or telling the other to go fetch some more paper rolls and markers. Now the words sit in our throats.

"These your sisters?"

"My nieces." She points to one of them, who is dressed

163

in a magenta and yellow outfit. "She's really smart. Takes after my sister-in-law."

For a brief instant, I wonder if Ishrat's parents have already arranged a marriage for her. She's my age, maybe even a year older. Though she told me she wants to finish her degree first. Go on to be a social worker. Why, I wonder, do I even care?

"I saw you the other day. Talking to Noor. You're really good with all the kids."

I feel a pinch of guilt. "Thanks."

"In group, what you get out of them. You don't let them stay on the surface. You dig down to the hard feelings."

"It's nothing." I shrug. "Just some stuff I learned from acting."

"You going to do that acting class? The kids would love it."

"I guess." I pause. "You know what happened to Noor?"

She shrugs. "Her parents said they'd rather she stay home."

I remember how pale Noor became when I asked her about the website. I scared her off. "Are your parents like that?" I blurt out.

Ishrat laughs, hugging her elbows to her chest. "You must be kidding. My mother? She was a singer in college and used to hang around the Alliance Française smoking cigarettes and talking cinema. Anything European was better." She adds, "It was me who decided to cover my head."

"Really?"

"In high school I decided. My parents, they didn't care.

Maybe even they'd rather I didn't. Not to draw attention to myself."

"So why did you?"

She stiffens, lifting her chin. "It's not the same as it was for my parents. They belonged, back home. They could watch Bengali and French cinema and talk politics or skip a lecture or kiss in a park after dark. Basically everyone knew who they were. Middle-class kids, rebelling a little.

"But us? Forget it. How can we ever feel like we belong when we're treated like would-bes?" She tugs on the edge of her scarf. "I do this to let them know. It's who I am. Take it or leave it, right?" She slaps her thighs, straightens. "Well. Now you know all about me." I hear that trace of a Brooklyn accent curling her vowels—tough and hurt at the same time. It's so familiar. We've all got that in us.

For the first time I see how strong Ishrat is: her broad shoulders drawn back, an almost muscular fierceness beneath her dress. I never would have guessed her parents were once college sophisticates smoking cigarettes. But that's what it's like for us: we're the little pots that got smashed up in our family's journey over. We've got to pick up the pieces, with different accents, make ourselves new. Hope the cracks don't show. I know I should go fetch my stepmother and brother, but it's nice, just standing here under the branching shade. Ishrat's nieces are weaving in and out of the trees, their colorful outfits like vivid flames, shaking their wrists so their glass bangles tinkle.

She leans toward me. "Who's that?"

"Who?"

165

"That guy." She gives a little shake of her head. "That one. He's staring at us."

Across a stretch of grass, under another stand of trees, is a thin figure. He's holding his arms across his chest, cupping his elbows. Our eyes catch before he looks away. But the profile is familiar: light lashes stroking down on a pale cheek, uneven long nose. He's wearing a maroon kurta over jeans. When he turns back, his face catches under the streetlamp: haggard, more gaunt than I remember.

Ibrahim.

A furious racket starts up in my chest. *Ibrahim?* The guy who left me standing by that pinball arcade of alarms, pink and blue shirts fanning out of my backpack? Who set my whole life in a different direction?

"Ibrahim!" I call out.

He drops his arms and starts moving away, stumbling a little on the tree roots.

"Ibrahim, wait!" I half run, reach out, grab the tail of his shirt and tug. He twists around, surprised. We stare at each other. He looks different, his eyes two blots of shadow, his cheeks hollow. I've still got some shirt clumped in my fist.

"Naeem." Then he embraces me, patting me warmly. "*Asalamu alaikum!* How are you?"

My jaw goes tense. "Where've you been?"

"Around."

"I tried calling you—" I stop. All around, families are greeting one another, parents scooping up their children. *No*, I tell myself. *It's Eid. I can't get angry here.*

"What happened to you?" I ask instead.

Ibrahim leans closer and grasps both my shoulders. "I was not myself," he whispers, and the whole time I can't stop staring at his eyes: they are light-colored, darker at the edges. It gives him a sad, gentle look.

"I did many things," he repeats. "I wasn't myself."

I can't believe this: Ibrahim at prayers? Ibrahim's been many things: Club boy. Wannabe business consultant. Manager for me. But never devout.

"I'll call you," he whispers in my ear. Before I can say anything more, he's slipped into the milling crowd. I'm so stunned I can't move. Ishrat has come up beside me.

"Who was that guy?" she asks.

"A friend," I say dully.

"I get a weird vibe off him."

"Yeah," I whisper. Still I don't move. Cars honk; the crowd is moving thickly toward the street. It's all I can do to watch the little girls spinning round and round the tree trunk, their ribboned braids a shiny blur.

CHAPTER 17

THE PHONE DINGS, REALLY LATE. A TEXT MESSAGE. I'M SPRAWLED out on my bed, sleep-heavy from the big meal Amma made for Eid Ul-Fitr. Crabs again, and deep-fried peppers, and *luchis,* perfect bread ovals that pop with sweet steam. My favorite. I'm sure she made them for me. After, trays of *sandesh,* milk sweets, cut on a slant, layered with silver foil, trembling cups of milky chai. Friends came and went all through the day; we ate and drank until we could have no more. Now the living room is littered with steel tumblers and glass teacups smudged with fingerprints.

Zahir is already asleep, curled shrimplike under his sheet. One of his presents was a big terry-cloth Spider-Man towel, and it's draped over his covers. The apartment lies still: dishes scraped, cleaned, and stacked on the drainboard. Zahir's new sneakers with fluorescent laces ready by the door.

I figure it must be Taylor, though he rarely texts me at this hour. Disoriented, I pull the phone from my side table.

The screen glows, showing an unfamiliar number. *Sorry bout bf. Had to go.*

Who is this?

A pause. The silver-blue rectangle flickers: *Ibrahim.*

My hands start to twitch. *Where are you??*

Busy.

Meet?

Soon. Inshallah. It will happen.

Furious, I tap: *When? Where?* But the screen has gone blank. I flop back down on my bed. I keep seeing Ibrahim under the shadowy tree branches; I can feel his fingers tightly gripping my arms. *I wasn't myself,* he'd whispered. His breath had been sour, his cheeks rough with a new beard. But I don't believe this devout business. I'm sure he's faking it, just like me. He has to be.

Now I definitely can't sleep; my mind pulses, anxious. Tossing off the sheet, I put on my jeans. Just as I'm slipping toward the door, I hear Zahir call out, "Where are you going?" His eyes are like tiny flashlight heads, combing the walls.

"Out."

He's up now, considering, his cheek tracked with creases, resting on an elbow. "Your job?"

"No. Not now." I wince. I've been thinking about this

169

a lot recently. I've never really explained to my family what I do, how it is I come home with clumps of money that I leave tucked between the salt and pepper shakers.

"What's your job?"

"A friend of mine. His dad has an electronics shop. I help out."

"Can I come sometime?"

I bend over and rumple his hair. "Someday, sure."

"What about Taslima-auntie? Do you work for her too?"

I hesitate. Should I tell him the truth? "I help out there too. You know. Community stuff."

"Is that where you're going now?"

"No." I feel a dry exasperation rising up in me. But this is the way Zahir is—he latches on to something and he won't let go. He sits for hours poring over the charts of the Avengers, trying to figure out what happened when.

I laugh, patting the sheet. "Go to sleep, Zahir. Give your brain a rest."

Once outside, I head toward Seventy-Third Street, where the air is carnival-soft, melted pastel. People are out; cars move sluggishly on Roosevelt Avenue. Each store is a blazing lozenge of light, candy-bright. Strands of tiny blue bulbs wink in the tree branches. Young wives with their husbands, still out from celebrating, totter on strappy high heels, clutching their beaded purses. Some of the old men are sitting at the outdoor tables, chewing paan or nursing chai in paper cups. Everyone can feel it: how after the prayers, the fast, the relief lets go into the summer night.

Only I can't touch it. I'm whirring and confused, thinking of Ibrahim. What I felt before—me, a winged protector—has been peeled off. I'm brought back to my raw beginning: the evening at the mall, three lousy shirts in my backpack. The bleeping alarms. Taylor and Sanchez in a rain-smelling car, the bag of weed. How did I get here? Maybe it's the long days of fasting and then eating too much today. No. It's seeing Ibrahim under the shifting shadows of the leaves by the masjid.

I bump through the crowds, lost. The old men, their hennaed beards and hair glaring like copper, don't like me. They know I'm an outsider, a crack in the flawless glass of night. A family in a restaurant leans in to each other, laughing. Their eyes slide over me. They know. I used to be one of them.

Someone taps me on the arm. "Hey."

I jerk backward. It's Jamal with his poufed-out hair and braces. I can't believe a kid who's eighteen still has braces. He's grinning wide. "Naeem!"

"Hi," I say feebly. I'm amazed that he's being so nice to me. "How are you doing?"

"Workin' a lot at the store."

I wince, thinking about how I used him for my lie to my family about my job. I remember suddenly how the two of us used to save up coins we'd scoop from our parents' bureaus and buy plastic water guns. Then we'd go to the little stretch of concrete in the back of his building and squirt ourselves silly. One time we got in trouble because we accidentally soaked an old man who was here from Kolkata visiting his daughter. Amma boxed my ears, then put me in fresh clothes and made me and Jamal deliver a package of sweets as an apology. The old man, who was very lonely, was so glad to see us.

"Gotta sign up for classes soon. Hope I'll get the programming ones." He adds, "You still taking that class?"

I nod, about to tell him more, when someone shouts, "Hey, Jamal! We gotta go! *Chalo,* man!"

Behind Jamal a group of guys is shifting under the awning of a cell phone store. I recognize some faces— Sameer, Ashik. In years past, for Eid Ul-Fitr, after we ate at home, we'd head out to meet our friends. Sometimes the girls would join, still in their stiff, starched outfits. Or we'd break onto a rooftop. Firecrackers popped in the distance. I could see Manhattan, the city a twinkling code to master. Then we scattered, one by one, to different paths.

They wave. But there's some kind of hard divide between us.

He smiles, embarrassed. "I should go."

He headed back to the others. In the fall he'll be off to City College, to programming classes, a future I can't imagine. An ache spreads hard in my chest. I'd give anything to be him. To worry about registration, some job, and how to pay for my textbooks.

There's a buzzing in my pocket. The phone lights up with a new message from Taylor. *What do you have?*

I don't answer, but turn back into the night, wondering how I got here and what happens next.

CHAPTER 18

A FEW SUMMERS AGO, I WAS WOKEN BY A CALL IN THE MIDDLE OF the night. I heard my father shouting into the receiver, as he always does, as if he doesn't trust a telephone to carry what he means. Especially when it's an overseas call. He used to do the same when I was still in Dhaka and we'd Skype: he'd lean toward the screen, his nose and eyes enlarged, his face distorted. To him, nothing—words, computers—can ever bridge the distance between people.

After that call I could hear my stepmother crying in the bedroom. Her father, who had moved back to Bangladesh several years before, had just died. There were more calls and whispers into the morning hours. Then she was gone, with Zahir.

Abba and I lived like two bachelor brothers. Neighbors and friends came and dropped off dishes, spoons balanced on the cover plates. Abba managed the store pretty well; I helped in the afternoons. Evenings Abba and I would either eat the boiled rice and dal and fish left for us or we'd go to a kebab house and watch soccer and cricket games.

But the hot days grew harder, longer. I couldn't bear to watch another TV show or listen to his complaints about the store or the piles of paperwork, which Amma usually handled. I began to make excuses about plans at night. When I stepped from the shower, doused in cologne, my hair gelled into spikes, Abba glared at me. I was an affront to his orderly but pained life.

"Restless," Abba would grumble. "Always so restless, this boy. Why must you go out all the time?"

"I just do."

Early in the morning, I could hear Abba arguing with my stepmother on Skype. He wanted her back. The store, it was too much. I was too much. He needed her to make the doctors' appointments and fill out the school forms for me and Zahir, to take over handling me, the strange creature he could not comprehend. She tearfully agreed.

The weekend before Amma was to return with Zahir, Abba abruptly announced that on our day off, a Sunday, we were going to Rockaway to go fishing.

I groaned. I still had hours of sleep ahead of me. I dove my face into my pillow. "Abba, no! Not today! Please!"

He tapped me once on the soles of my feet, told me I was not to bring my cell phone, pointed to the shower, and that was that. By the time I'd had my breakfast he'd already dragged out his fishing rod and a cooler, where he'd put bottles of ice water and rutis and potatoes in foil.

I was embarrassed on the bus, Abba sitting erect on the seat, holding his rod like a spear. The other passengers glanced, laughed; a little boy pointed until his grandmother slapped his wrist.

We emerged from the ride sweaty, stinking of fumes. He bought a few plastic bags of bait and then we made our way along the beach, stepping around the sunbathers. He told me nothing—where we were going, how long we would be. I traipsed behind, thinking about how I could be on the handball court instead of here.

Abba walked to a jetty made of stones heaped up in overlapping piles. Balancing the empty bucket and rod, he slipped every now and then in his rubber sandals, then regained his balance. I carried our small cooler. He sat down at a far end, wedging an empty plastic bucket into a seam in the rocks.

We said nothing.

I was furious at first, thinking, *Just like him. He doesn't say anything. He just expects me to just be.*

For a while I sullenly tossed stones into the ocean, or I wandered up and down the slick jetty, staring at the pretty girls in bikinis, their flat stomachs shiny with lotion. My father was a still figure, casting his rod, occasionally reeling it in.

When I returned, I saw only two wriggling fish in the bucket.

"That's all?" I asked.

"*Ra' Sono,*" he replied. Patience.

At lunchtime, we had finished off our supply of water and bought a bottle from a man who wheeled and bumped his covered cart across the sand. He kissed the dollar bill we gave him and then made the sign of the cross. We drank it down with our rutis and potatoes, which were cold from the cooler. Then Abba resumed his fishing from another rock.

I was surprised to find that my impatience had settled. The sun beat on the back of my neck, but it was not unpleasant. A good wind blew at us. Sometimes Abba would let out a laugh as he pulled in a fish, grappling with the breeze rippling across his long shirt, throwing him off balance. I occupied myself digging out old bottle caps and collected them in a stack for Zahir. I arranged some worn glass shards too. Abba spoke, nodding approvingly. "When you were little, you were this way," he said. "So resourceful. For hours you played by yourself. Your mother and I were so surprised and amazed."

I grinned.

"You remind me of Rasul."

I started, the smooth glass in my palm. Abba never speaks about Rasul. Abba was the younger brother, the one left behind, who watched his mother fist the curtain and stare out at the street, praying, waiting for Rasul. Everyone knew the terrible stories: the villages torched, the boys who lost their eyes and limbs and youth. She didn't want a hero. She just wanted her son back. But in our family, when Rasul returned, he was not the same. *Funny in the head* is all my grandmother would say. *As if he never came back to us.*

"It's so easy," Abba remarked now.

"What's easy?" I asked.

He thought for a moment. "To forget what your true nature is."

Then he swung the rod over his head and said no more until late afternoon, when he had finally caught a good number of fish, sealed the bucket with a punctured top, and gathered up his rod.

"There," he said. "We take this back and clean it for your mother for tomorrow."

And that's how I understood how he wanted me to remember this day. Abba didn't trust words or Skype or computers. He trusted only these, the small tasks that matter: Bait on a hook. My collection of bottle caps and glass. The man who kissed his dollar bill.

That day Abba showed me we must find ourselves wherever we are. And it will be all right.

CHAPTER 19

IN THE NEXT DAYS, I'M LIKE A TWIN ENGINE BORING DOWN, homed. I put in a few hours at the leadership camp. Then I'm back to checking out mosques, helping with the charity, delivering soup and pasta boxes. I'm sure Taylor's guys, filing away their reports somewhere in their maze of offices, must be getting a kick out of my pics. Woo-hoo. Serious stuff here. Campbell's Chicken and Stars soup. Some kind of message in that?

There are a lot of people coming and going. I even ask, "Have you seen a pale, skinny dude?"

One of the volunteers, bent over a box, straightens up. "He goes to Queens?"

"LaGuardia." Then I add, "Sometimes."

He shakes his head. "Doesn't ring a bell."

When I'm done, sometimes I stick around for evening

prayers. Or I walk, doing circles around the area. Used to be this neighborhood was considered kind of rough. But a few years ago, people began buying up houses. A few of Abba's friends tried to get him to join them. Now there are Bangladeshi restaurants and markets. A family we know owns a big brick house with two apartments, pulling in a good rent.

I text Ibrahim. Nothing.

A string of twenty-two messages, all unanswered. I don't care. There's a slow burn in me. I want him to know I'm not the same Naeem. Not the dumb sucker who just followed along where his words led. Not the kid who dropped his old friends or took the heat for some stupid shirts. He owes me.

I walk and walk, even in the heat, staring up at those satellite dishes perched on roofs, trying to see right through the milky nylon curtains. Maybe because my parents always talked about this neighborhood in hushed tones, I'm sure there's trouble.

Somewhere, someone's on the Internet, on the wrong site, going the bad way.

Somewhere in there is Ibrahim.

Sunday afternoon: quiet in the store. The only sound is the rip-rip of cardboard—my X-Acto knife slicing open taped boxes. The air here is dim, a rectangular slab of light just barely reaching me in the back.

The new supplies have arrived—paper and nice pens, five dollars for two; folders and Post-its and envelopes.

Amma had a new sign made up: *School & Office Supplies Here!* She's bought rotating wire racks with baskets, for highlighters and Scotch tape. The copier will be installed on Monday.

Abba stands outside, fiddling with the new backpacks on rollers that they display in front of the store, a metal chain looped through their handles. A little girl walks by with her grandmother, who often comes into the store. Abba warmly puts his hand on her head as she starts to ride the little mechanical painted pony next door, her skirt flaring around her knees.

I promised myself to stick with helping in the store so it will be ready for Monday, when we have a rush. There's just this: the sound of cardboard flapping open; another package slid on a shelf. Later I'll finish my essay, the last one for this course. Like prayer, my work for Taylor, the help with Taslima. I'm fastened to something small, steady.

I don't hear the text-ding the first time.

Let's hang. I.

I pause, packets in hand. The tips of my fingers tingle. I stare at the unfinished boxes. No. I'm not letting him do this to me.

You there?

Another box. Each like a spike of energy, my fix.

Abba peeks his head in the store doorway. Even with the sunlight streaming in, backlighting his head, I can see a slight furrow in his brow. "Everything good, Naeem?"

A shot of guilt. "Yes, Abba."

"You'll get it done today?"

"Yes."

"Bhalo," he says. Good.

I set the X-Acto knife down. Just a message. *Yeah.*

The answer comes in a flash. *Come hang.*

I hesitate. *Where?*

The phone lights up: *Exxon Station. Hillside Ave. Near 170th.*

My ears pulse. My palms are wet. Abba will kill me. But I can't stop myself. I've got to get out of here, back out on the damp and glaring streets, finding Ibrahim. Finding what I need to know.

CHAPTER 20

EVEN FROM ACROSS THE STREET, I SPOT HIM.

A thin figure, hopping from car to car at the full-service island, sliding the credit cards. Ibrahim pumping gas? The guy trying on a suit three months ago is in a mechanic's blue coverall, smiling as he hands a card back to a driver.

"Ibrahim," I call.

When he turns around, his face shows gladness, worry. *"Asalamu alaikum,"* he calls.

"Alaikum asalam."

"How are you?"

He embraces me, but I go stiff under his thumping hands. "Good," I mumble. "You?"

As he steps back, I see that his hair curls a little in the humidity. A patch of discolored skin shows near his ear, which I never noticed before. "It's a bitch. Friend of mine broke his leg, so I'm filling in." He shakes his head. "Serious setback."

On the subway over, walking the blocks from the stop, I raked this over in my head. How I'd slug him in the jaw, throw him flat on his back. But it's weird. Ibrahim's greeting me as if we hung in his car last night. He's happy to see me.

"Wanna get a bite? I can take a break now. Catch up."

"I guess."

My heart is thumping hard as I follow him into the little office, where he's stripping off the mechanic suit, fast. It's dirty, stiff with grease, sitting in peaked curves on the floor. Underneath he's wearing the same kurta I saw that night at the mosque over a pair of jeans.

He calls to another man over in the mechanic shop, an old Punjabi, who shuffles forward with slow, wary steps. The man mutters something in Urdu, which I can't understand; they argue a few minutes. "My friend's uncle," Ibrahim explains as we head out. "He doesn't know how to close out the shift. Gets confused about the credit cards sometimes. Doesn't want me to leave him here."

"I can come later."

"No, no, man. That's what sucks about being a manager. Gotta do everything!"

I feel dubious that Ibrahim is a manager, but it's as it always was—the half-truths, a custardy glide of words. *Don't fall for it,* I tell myself.

We walk several blocks to a joint where we order chicken and rice. I'm watchful, trying to figure out who he really is.

He seems like the same old Ibrahim, leaning tight toward me, laughing as he grabs my Fanta soda and sucks it down. His eyes are soft. "How *are* you?" he asks, worried, as if I'm the one who disappeared off the face of the earth.

"Okay." There's a nervous thrumming in the pit of my stomach, like a snare drum. I keep waiting for him to say something. About that night. The mall. Leaving me stranded. Or what's kept him from calling.

"What've you been up to?" he asks.

"Summer school."

"That's a drag."

"And you?" I line up the words, bead by bead.

His eyes flare. "Lots. Me and my uncles, we had a business we started. Great stuff—"

"What was it?" I remember him once mentioning an electronics and phone shop out on Long Island—they'd found some good space in a strip mall where the rents were cheap. "Wireless?"

"Wireless!" he laughs. "No, no." He wipes his mouth. "You know family politics. They'd rather spend more time arguing with each other." His knee starts to bounce up and down the way it used to. He can't stay still. "That's why I'm going out on my own. That's how to do it. Seize the opportunity."

Beneath the patter, he seems anxious. The plans that used to flow from him come in spurts. And his skin has that sallow color, as if he's been indoors a lot, under fluorescent lights. He looks unwashed, the collar of his shirt frayed.

"So you're working at a gas station?" I chew my meat slowly. It's tasteless.

He blushes. "For a while." He lapses into silence, takes a few stabs at his plate. "That's the thing, Naeem. It's not just what's in front of you. It's what you do in the long run." He offers a vague smile. "I've been reading, Naeem. Bettering myself."

"Bettering?"

"It's so easy to get seduced by the here and now. Temptation. Material. Stuff."

Like shoving three stolen shirts in my backpack? I want to yell. This is just Ibrahim weaseling out of things, as he always does. The fake Ray-Ban sunglasses he loved to draw off his face. Turning in that suit, jerking the cuffs by his wrist.

When Ibrahim shuffles his feet and jumps up from the table, something breaks inside me. This is what he always does. He dances from one place to another, and I follow. I go with his story, ride along. I reach over, grab his wrist and hold it tight. "Why didn't you call?"

He looks at me, surprised. "What do you mean?"

"I was texting you for days."

His eyes go foggy. "I told you, it's been crazy—"

"What about the last three months?"

I can see he's taken aback, even a little scared. I still have his wrist in my grip. I've never shown this kind of anger to him. But I am not letting him go. "That night? In the mall?"

He flinches. "Oh yeah. That."

"What were you doing? Putting those shirts in my back-pack?"

He shakes his head, helpless. "I told you. I wasn't myself. That wasn't me."

"It was you!" My chair bangs backward. A few of the other people in the restaurant pop up their heads. I tense. Don't make a scene: Two Muslim-looking kids. What will they think?

"It was a test, Naeem."

"A test?"

"Yes," he murmurs. "We all have tests." He gives me a bleary smile. "Now it's all good. You're here, aren't you? You've found your way to me."

I want to punch him across his jaw. Blurt out everything—the cops and the drive, Taylor and Sanchez. But I'm shaking so hard it's like I'm sick with a chill. The guy behind the counter—a heavyset Caribbean man flipping meat on a grill—gives us a warning look.

"Are you going to let me go?" he asks weakly. He pulls back his wrist and massages the skin. Then he shakes his head, as if I'm the crazy one.

We walk in silence. Me with my hands thrust in my pockets. I'm so angry I can't speak. How is it that none of it matters? *I* don't matter. He doesn't care. About me, about our friendship. He never did. Who was I kidding? I'm a tagalong who used to show up at the smallest text.

He's still got that Ibrahim energy—dancing forward on

the pavement, then back, then forward again. But it's like I'm coming out of a fog. A watchful sheath comes over me. I notice things. The beard. The inward look of his eyes. The odd way he shrinks back when a girl passes us in a tank top and cutoff shorts.

"You pray?" I ask.

"Yeah. Not every day." He adds proudly, "Haven't touched weed. Beer. Nothing."

I take this in. Don't say a word.

As we get close to the station, he puts his hand on my shoulder. "Later, man. Let's hang soon."

"I don't have your number."

He pulls out his phone and I notice it isn't his old phone. It's the kind you get at Target, preloaded, for fifty bucks. An instant later his number dings in my in-box. *Soon, bro! Peace be with you.* Then he rolls his eyes as if he's under some great burden, managing the station.

The Punjabi man meets Ibrahim halfway onto the lot, his elbows angled back. Even from here I can hear him yelling. This isn't about some goof-up with the cash register. He's furious. I watch for a while. I'm not letting him go.

A day after I saw him, Ibrahim's number didn't work. Two days later I go to the gas station; Ibrahim's not there. Now I know I have to follow through. Stupid mistake: leaving without even finding out where he lives. I want to throttle him. But I'm staying on this.

The Punjabi man is shaking his head. "Doesn't work

here. No more." He makes a small motion, as if to brush Ibrahim away.

"Do you know where he lives?"

"No work here. Don't know."

I walk away. How does Ibrahim do it? Always one step ahead of me. Then I stop, rub my temples. Focus. I go back to the gas station. I will not let him slip away from me like this. Not again.

The old guy is sorting bills at the register. His fingers look dry, wrinkled.

"I know you know," I say. "There's a problem. I need to get ahold of him."

The man hesitates.

"A big problem," I add.

Sighing, he lifts up the plastic tray and fishes out a scrap of paper. "He does not stay with family. Some apartment."

The handwriting is jagged. The paper glows like it's radioactive. Like I'm going to disappear, poof, the instant I touch it.

CHAPTER 21

IT'S NOT EVEN A REAL STREET. MORE A NARROW DRIVEWAY MADE tight with an SUV and a livery car. I just barely scrape past the side-view mirror to find a little door on the side of the house. No buzzer, so I rap my knuckles. From across the way, over a metal fence, a woman who is pinning up her laundry stares at me. "Knock hard!" she yells. "They have TV on loud there!"

Turns out the door is open, the hallway ceiling so low that the people upstairs seem to be walking right on my head. At the very end there's another door, also open. Inside, a small room with a massive TV, filling the air with blue aquarium light. Everything swims before me seaweed-tangled. I can just make out a mound of DVD cases on the floor, a small table with a computer. And Ibrahim, sitting on a futon, his elbows on his knees.

He looks up, his face creased in a tired smile. "Hey! How'd you find me?"

"Hey." I sit down beside him, hear the futon creak. "I stopped by the gas station."

His expression darkens. "That's over."

"What happened?"

He shrugs. "Crappy place. Not worth it." He turns and I notice his eyes are bloodshot. I wonder if he's been dipping back into weed.

"Busy?" I ask.

"Nah."

We sit there, awkward. I don't like how he spoke as if he's on some remote mountaintop, far above, peering down, me the kid. He's trying to make me small. Doesn't he know? I'm the one at the higher altitude. I jerk up from the futon, check out his belongings, loiter by the computer, try to see if there are any sites to note.

"Wanna smoke?"

He smiles. His teeth are small, yellow. "Weed?"

"Yeah. Last I heard that's what it's called."

He gives a scowl, like the one he gave that girl on the street the other day. Then he shakes his head, wistful. "That's not good, Naeem. You need to get your life together. Not put those poisons in your body."

My eyes rove the small room: a pizza box next to the computer, a few crusts furry with mold. Laundry mashed in a corner.

"So what's up with you?" he asks.

"Same. School. Finishing this class. Next up is pre-cal. Then I can get my degree."

"Good luck with that," he scoffs.

I feel a burn. "What's that supposed to mean?"

"All that is bullshit. They just keep you like a little rat, chasing after nothing. What's a degree but a load of debt? Colleges, universities, they're just money machines selling thoughts you can have yourself. You know what they say. Those who can, do. Those who can't, take classes." Then he adds, "And those who really can't do anything teach."

"My teacher's really good."

This makes him curious. "She like you?"

I flush, thinking of Professor Emily jumping around the room, how she's not afraid to write across the top of the page *You know better. You can do better. Proof!* Slowly I'm working at it, trying a little more. The last one I pulled a B–. "Yeah, I think so."

"Just keep an eye on that. Don't let her cut you down, man. Mess with your head."

In the old days, I would have joined Ibrahim in his put-down. Isn't that what we used to do? Huddle at a diner, tell stories about our teachers giving us a hard time. He'd egg me on, tell me to flash my Naeem straight-teeth smile. Now his comment makes me angry. It's like looking at myself through the wrong end of a telescope, from an earlier time: puny, with veins of meanness.

"I had a teacher like that once," Ibrahim goes on. "She

was hot. She took me aside. I think she had a thing for me. But you know what I found out?"

"What?"

"She was a total fake. Yelled at me in class. In front of everyone! Then she failed me. Over one stupid paper. Said I plagiarized, which is bull. I didn't do that. I filed a complaint. How unprofessional she was. The whole thing was a setup."

"What do you mean?"

He shakes his head. "You think a guy with my name is gonna win? No way."

This is new, a bitter turn I've never seen. Before, everything to Ibrahim was a great gliding game—you skated on the surface, you moved on. You didn't nurse a grudge. You didn't give them that power over you. Now he's a crabbed little guy with moldy pizza crust in a dark room.

"What'd you do?"

He laughs. "Fought it out with the dean. I could see he was in with her." He halts, pulls himself up short.

"But did you do it?"

He looks at me, shocked. "Dude, you too? Of course I didn't." But he doesn't sound so sure.

I'm confused. If he plagiarized, then it was his fault. But maybe the teacher, the dean did give him a hard time because he was a Muslim. I think about all the stories in the leadership camp. The girl who was jeered at on a subway for her head scarf. The graffiti on the wall of a mosque. Noor dumping her bag before the security guard. That anxious twist in the pit of your stomach every time there's another big news story about a terrorist. *It can make you crazy,* one of the kids said. Sometimes you're imagining it. Other times you're not.

"So what's next?" I ask.

"I have a plan," he says, and grins.

I shiver. "What plan?"

He laughs. "Oh, Naeem. You crack me up. 'What plan?'" he mimics. "What do you think? This is some kind of a little book report? A Power Point you do for extra credit? This is on another plane, brother. You have to go beyond what you know." He adds, "Beyond what most people think of you."

When he flips on the controller, there's contempt in his arms, his shoulders, as if to say *Join me if you want to, little guy.* I don't know how he does it. Even here, in this pathetic little room, in the same unwashed clothes, Ibrahim has a way of making me seem ordinary.

On the screen is *Far Cry,* a solo shooter game, paused midsequence. The sighter is trained on a valley, snowcapped ranges in the distance. Now he's bent forward, control in his hands, leaning into the game, steering the shooter around boulders and long grasses. Blowing open a steel box. Soon he's completely absorbed, shoulders, arms shaking as he aims at a figure in the distance. The game's over. He slams down the controller and looks up, wild-eyed, as if surprised to see me here.

And that's when I know.

Or I think I know.

It's the eyes: pin-bright, like imploded stars. A deadness inside. He doesn't see me. He sees through me, past me.

193

The light sifts down from the windows. For the first time I notice the screen on his computer. Opened to Islam-awake. "I better go," I say. I can't breathe. "Gotta pick up my little brother." I feel queasy, as if the floor is made of waves rolling beneath me.

He casts me a beatific smile. "Someday," he murmurs, "you'll see, Naeem. What I can do. There are always people holding you down. But I'll have my day."

"Yeah, sure," I mumble.

I leave. The whole trip back on the subway, I can't shake that scene: Ibrahim, hunched in front of a flashing screen, fingers tensed on the controller. That chilly ocean washing up under me. Tugging me deeper, into what I don't know.

I stand under the elevated line's slashing shadows, where I usually meet Taylor and Sanchez. I'm trembling like crazy, as if I've got a fever. I've got to blurt this out quick.

Taylor's on the other end of the line, waiting. I know he's surprised by my call.

"You want to know about lone wolves?" I finally say.

A pause. "Yeah."

A train passes; dirty water cascades down the flaking metal girders. I'm losing my nerve.

"Naeem?"

There's a distant whoosh, a train approaching. It stops in a tornado of noise. My mouth opens, shuts again.

"I have a friend."

CHAPTER 22

SANCHEZ.

Not on a stool, or in the back. Sitting right opposite me, in broad daylight, shaking his sugar packet into his coffee. Grinning. No dodge and fake here. No two-bit kid sitting in the shadows, pocketing bills. No sneaky walk in a strange neighborhood. I've moved up; I'm one of them. I'm redeemed in Sanchez's eyes. I got the stuff. It's like a reunion from that first night they took me to the diner.

It's been about a week. I've told them everything. About Ibrahim's computer. His strange talk. They've been able to do some intelligence on him. They picked up some kind of intercept. Postings. Chatter about family in Pakistan. *Time to join two parts,* one said. *No more feuds. We are one.*

But I don't know. It could be nothing. It could be what Ibrahim said—a squabble. A misunderstanding. Maybe he was serious about that online stuff. But that was Ibrahim, always deep in his head. Lost on the Internet. As usual, I don't have the big picture. I'm swimming too far down in the murk. I wish I knew for sure what Ibrahim meant.

"We need more," Taylor urges. "Did he say anything about what he's doing next?"

I keep turning Ibrahim's words over, trying to remember, trying to understand. But there's no understanding. Just that uneasy feeling in his apartment. His paranoid talk. And his eyes. And this: my chance to set things right. Dude didn't even admit to what he did to me. What do I owe him? Nothing.

"He's planning something," I blurt out.

A look flashes between them. "Go on," Taylor says.

"I can't say what. But he says it's big."

I feel the air go taut.

"He give you specifics?"

"No."

Again the silent conference between these two.

"Look, it might be nothing. Probably just some family drama."

"No doubt," Sanchez says.

We fall silent. I feel sick and cold and sick again. "Maybe he's just mixed up."

"Maybe," Taylor concedes. "But you want to take a chance?"

I shrug. I don't know what to say.

"Naeem." Taylor's looking at me, straight on. "Get real. He's the guy who left you in the lurch."

"Yeah," I manage.

"That sucks. He a friend of yours from school?"

I shake my head. "No. Around."

"What about his family? Who he hangs with?"

I shake my head again. "I don't know. It's like we had this thing. We'd hang around, just with each other."

"A loner," Sanchez observes.

I wince. "I guess."

"See?" Taylor's hands are splayed. "You never know a person. Not really."

"Sucks," Sanchez echoes.

My mood has gone gray. I know I should be jumping with joy. Finally! I showed them. Gave them a solid lead. But there's an unease twitching underneath my thoughts. I'm not sure about Ibrahim. Is he going over to the other side? I don't know. I know what I've been pushing away all these months, doing better in my life, rising up to skim air, sun. Underneath, though, there was this dark cave of hurt. Not the one with Abba, with Ibrahim. I couldn't understand why he cut me like that.

"That's what I'm trying to tell you, Naeem. In this line of work, you never know. Someone can be one way on the outside. But inside"—he shakes his head—"whew."

Sanchez grins. "But now you got to hang with us."

"Yeah, great," I mumble.

"You know the conveyor belt theory?" asks Taylor.

I shake my head, tired. I want this conversation to be over.

"Someone's on it, heading toward radicalization. It's where we catch them, before they can do damage."

"So what do you want me to do?"

"Push it harder. Keep up the conversation. Ask him his feelings about the government. Keep it going. Ask if you can help. Say you know people. That you're fed up too."

"But isn't that, like, trapping him?"

"It's procedure," Sanchez puts in crisply.

"Okay." After all, I'm the one who told them about Ibrahim. What did I think would happen? That they would take him off my hands? Of course not. I'm in deeper than I was before. I check my watch. It's time for me to get back to the store and help Abba. "That it? You going to pay me?"

A glance between the two of them. I can feel the frustration boiling up inside me. I hate this—their little tease with money. It's never straightforward.

"There is one thing. An item—"

"What?" I ask, irritated. I just want to leave, pocket my bills, and later sort out the questions sloshing inside me.

"A wire," Sanchez confirms.

A small prickle at the back of my neck. This is more than I bargained for. But it's exciting, too.

Then he reaches into his pocket. It's tiny as can be, encased in black plastic, resting in his palm. It looks kind of like a Bluetooth, only the clip is different.

"You understand?"

A puckering in the air, drawing us close, secret.

I can see Ibrahim's haggard look, blots of shadow under his eyes. Is that who I wanted to catch? But maybe they're right. Ibrahim is plotting something. This is my chance. To do something for real. Slip a tiny device inside my shirt.

Talk smooth, so he doesn't even notice where I'm leading. Set the trap.

"Do I have to?" I ask.

"It's the only way," Sanchez replies.

"Naeem?"

It's Zahir, his eyes shining like an insect's in the dark.

"Hey," I whisper. "What's wrong?"

He's rubbing his eyes with his fists. "I had a bad dream."

As I sit down on the edge of his bed, he flings his arms around my neck and presses against me, trembling. I feel his thin ribs against mine, his breaths panicked and fast.

"What kind of dream?" I ask. His neck smells tangy-orange, of soap and shampoo.

"I don't know. There's this country. No, not a country, it's a world. A planet. They're on the ceiling. They want to take me away. They want me to go with them."

I get up and pour him a glass of water from the bathroom sink, which he gulps, his lips parched. His eyes are fever-bright wicks, which scares me. Every now and then this happens. He sleepwalks and stutters about alternate worlds and people and numbers chasing him. Zahir's always been a light sleeper, hypersensitive to noise and light. He hears and sees things, and then they rise in him, an insistent chain of words.

"Hey," I tease. "What about those math books? Have you been working on them?"

"Some," he says. "But I need you."

I laugh. "You know how bad I am at math. You're the whiz."

He slips his hand into my palm, his voice tiny. "Will you help me?"

"Sure," I say.

"You won't."

"Zahir," I say, getting a little impatient. "I told you. I will." I pat the covers. "It's time to go to sleep."

"Where are you going all the time? Why can't you just stay?"

I slide my arms around his thin shoulders, hold him to me. "Nowhere," I whisper.

Eventually I feel him give way, his little body releasing. His breathing grows long, steady. I gently tuck him back in, smooth the covers over his quieted limbs.

Then I see: he was working on the desk that sits between our two narrow beds. The math book I bought for him is opened. But so is my computer. When I go to shut it down, the hairs on the back of my hand tickle.

At least a half-dozen windows open on my screen. Sites, all the ones I know, the ones I follow for Taylor. I did not leave them open. I never leave them open.

But then again, I've been so freaked about the Ibrahim situation, maybe I did.

One by one, I point the arrow in the corner, click so they vanish. But even after they're all closed, I can't stop shaking.

I don't know how to stop this.

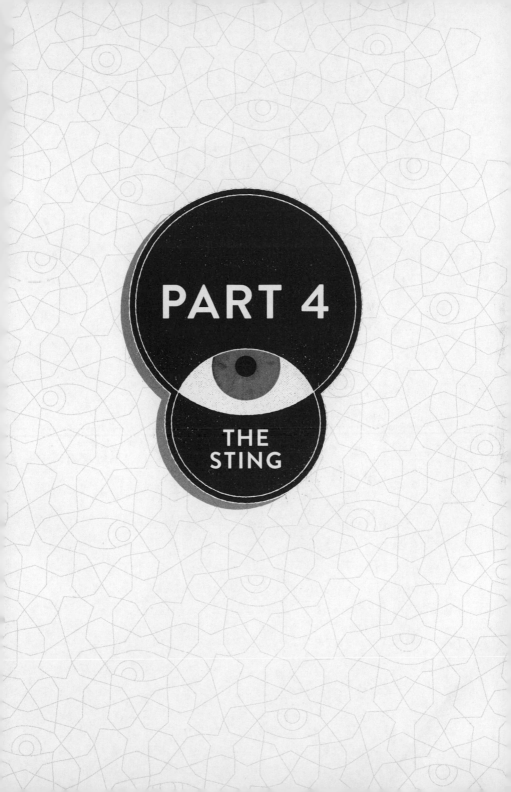

PART 4

THE STING

FILE

Subject: Ibrahim Syed, 19 years old
Address: Unknown. Presently residing at XXXX 165th Street, Jamaica, NY
DOB: XXXXXXXX
SSN: XXXXXXXXX
Mosque: Queens Islam Center

- Inquiry indicates that Ibrahim Syed is a frequent contributor to a Salafist Web forum called IslamAwake.com that is primarily for an English-speaking audience. This forum has been affiliated with the teachings of individuals who have been associated with individuals engaged in terrorism or criminal activity related to terrorism. Syed has posted before and after significant speeches telecast on the website.
- Attended LaGuardia Community College but is no longer enrolled.
- Landlord's name not obtained. Residence last occupied by several unidentified men of South Asian descent.
- Initial information obtained from neighbors describes erratic behavior and isolation from family. Family members travel to Pakistan with some regularity.

Plan of Action

- Subpoena phone records and submit for analysis.
- Continue surveillance.
- Pole camera request at corner of 165th Street.
- Mail cover request.

CHAPTER 23

THE SUN IS A WOBBLING SPOT IN THE SKY. ANOTHER BLAZING HOT August day. The apartment is humming with all the fans that are on. Abba is already in the living room; he has just finished his prayers. He rises, folds his prayer rug away in the closet. His shirt is patched with sweat.

Why do I always feel so flimsy next to my father? Even with the money I brought in last night—five hundred dollars! Only Abba is solid in the world.

Abba, I want to say. The question burns in my mouth. *What should I do?* But we don't talk like that.

"You are coming today to the store?" he asks.

"I have to work." My stomach tightens. I'm supposed to meet Taylor, get my instructions.

He shuffles to the refrigerator, snaps open the door, and retrieves the tubs of rice and kitchrie he and Amma will eat behind their counter today. The new stock is moving—they even had to order some more manila folders.

Ask him. Ask him. I'm sure my heart's going to explode out of my chest.

"Abba, was there ever a time when you had to do something . . . and you weren't sure if it was right?"

His eyebrows bristle, suspicious. "Somebody ask you for a bribe?"

"No, Abba."

"Bribe I never do."

"I know, Abba. It's not that." This is what Abba always talks about! As if we're still in Bangladesh. I don't know how to explain that that's not the way it is here. That's not what matters. "I mean . . . like being asked to do something against a friend."

He goes into gruff silence, stares at his feet. He takes so long I wonder if he's forgotten the question. After a while he looks up, his eyes squinted small. "This question is not a question," he says. "No one makes you do something. You do it. You. Do not act as if it is someone else. One time they asked me to do a bribe. I said no. I said no again. But then my mother said, we have no choice. But that is not true. We do have a choice. Even if I do something bad, even if I do it because it helps my family, or me, it is my choice."

To my surprise, my breath is still, caught in my throat. That's more advice than my father has ever given to me. Ever.

Grunting, he moves toward the hall. "Long day, hanh?" I hear the front door shut.

I almost run after him. *Abba!* I want to call. I want to be little like Zahir, full of terror and love, able to fling my arms around my father's waist, hard.

Outside, the heat hits me like an aluminum pan right between the eyes. The streets are all glare and heat. My lashes feel singed. After a couple of blocks, I duck into a little bodega and suck down a cold Coke under the slanted shade of an awning, where I was told to wait.

An Asian lady stands next to me, using an umbrella for the sun. Her skin is tinted milky-pink from the bowed red nylon.

"Bus comes here?" she asks.

"I think so." I shift uncomfortably. It's too hot to go any farther, out of the shade.

"I wait for bus. Always late." She looks at me curiously. "You are waiting for bus?"

"No. A friend."

"Lucky you. I have factory, but bus always late."

I know, lady, I think. *You said that already.* The heat's drilling a bit into my skull. Where is Taylor? I'll get my wire and instructions, then I'm off. I just want this to be over.

Taylor's car glides up. His sunglasses bounce with light. Sanchez is beside him, wolfing down what looks like an Egg McMuffin.

"Morning!" He grins.

"Morning!" The woman smiles, as if he's talking to her.

"You've got a friend," Taylor observes as I climb in beside him.

207

We turn off the main thoroughfare, where the slow-moving pedestrians are suspended in the sun's glaze. Taylor's car bumps on broken asphalt. "Listen, buddy. I was thinking. This must be kinda hard for you," he says.

"It is."

"Talk to me." That voice, like a father's, knowing.

The tight pain in my temples loosens just a little. "What if Ibrahim . . . doesn't take up on what I'm saying?"

He laughs. "We've got other fish to fry, Naeem. You think the department wants to waste all its resources on some kid fooling around on the Internet?"

I grin, despite myself. "I guess not."

"That's the spirit. If it's a bust, we've got other work for you."

This cheers me. I sink back into the seat, watch how Taylor's got his hand on the wheel, as if we have all the time in the world. Now we're steering down narrow streets of low aluminum-sided houses, then a boxy lineup of warehouses and garages.

Taylor pulls the car to the side, shuts off the ignition. He reaches into the glove compartment and pulls out a black nub of plastic. The wire. Leaned over the console between the two front seats, he shows me how to clip the device to my jeans waistband. It feels cool and hard against my bare skin. With his thumb, he flicks a small swatch of thick electrical tape to keep it fixed against my stomach.

"Here's the deal. You wear this. When you're done with your day, we take it off you. We put it on and pull it off. You never touch it. Never walk off with a wire, understand?"

"Don't even *think* about going anywhere," Sanchez adds. "Showing it off to your pals—"

There's heat on my face. "I wouldn't do that!"

Taylor settles back in the driver's seat. "Okay, now we're gonna go meet someone special."

"Aren't we driving to his place?" I can't even say Ibrahim's name out loud.

"We've got some agency cooperation here. FBI." He adds, "Another guy. So you don't have to do all the heavy lifting."

"I don't understand."

"It's like me and Sanchez. We're a team. Yin and yang and all that."

What about you and me? I want to say.

"This guy is the best," he says as he starts the car and makes a right on the next street. "Experienced. He knows what he's doing. He'll be your backup. You lay the foundation. Once you get Ibrahim warmed up, the idea is you introduce him as your friend. He's the one with the connections, who can help with the plan. He'll take it from there."

A hundred questions crowd my mind. Is this really happening—FBI? A partner? We've drawn up to a place where rows of gleaming hubcaps are stacked against a wall. Several cars are jacked up on lifts. From inside the warehouse a guy moves toward us, wiping his hands on a rag. Something about him is familiar. The thick crop of wavy black hair. The sloped shoulders. I blink. It can't be.

Tareq.

CHAPTER 24

Tareq.

Tareq, the Bangla guy my parents always whisper about. Shady. Trouble. Dirty-mouthed. Stay away from him. The one Taslima doesn't like. Why didn't I get it that time by her car? The way he eyed me.

Tareq, leaning into the car, grinning. Tareq, looking like a grizzled tiger, as he always does: thick-pawed, shaggy hair, a gold-hued face. "Hey, Naeem."

"Hey." I can barely make the word crawl out of my throat.

"He's going to help you out, man. Knows what to do."

For a brief second, I wish I could tell my little brother. *Hey, Zahir, man, I'm on the inside of an undercover plot— can you believe it? Just like one in our books!* "Cool," I say.

"Very cool," Tareq agrees.

I keep looking at him for a signal. For him to burst out laughing at the joke. The coincidence. How many times was I at some party where he was in a corner of the room, boasting, talking bull? Or I saw him leaned up against his car outside our high school, a pretty girl combing her hair in the passenger seat.

He acts like this is the most normal thing in the world. "You ready?"

"I guess."

"All you got to do is set it up," Taylor explains.

"Poke," Tareq says with a grin.

"Poke?"

"You poke a little bait in the water. The hungry fish, he's gonna take it. I promise. Pretty soon it's on the line." He adds to me: *"Noro na, mach eibar kamracche."* Steady, the fish is now biting.

"You got it, buddy?" Taylor asks.

"Yes," I say. I have the quivering sensation of being handed off into air. I'm leaving the secret cave of Taylor's car and everything we've done together: basketball, doughnuts, café con leche. Suddenly I'm on a whole other level. This is real.

"Have fun, boys," Sanchez laughs as we walk down an alley. He stops before a blue BMW.

"Whoa," I say. "That's sick."

"Whoa is right."

More questions nag at me. But he's already inside, pulling off his T-shirt and grabbing a collared shirt, taking out the pins and cardboard. He runs a comb through his thick hair so it waves back around his ears, and checks his teeth in the visor mirror.

"What are you doing? Get in."

Sheepish, I slip into the passenger seat. The car is clean, chemical-smelling. New rubber mats. I run my palm over the buttery leather seats, the gray piping.

"You don't seem like the usual cut of guys we get," he remarks. "Usually they're stoners. Or lowlifes. Like me."

"You're not—"

"Quit it," he interrupts. With his mashed-up T-shirt in his hand, he swivels out of the car, opens the trunk. For a moment every bad TV cop show I've watched with Abba flashes before me, and I'm sure he's going to come back with an assault rifle. The trunk slams, making the car shudder. It's just Tareq, though, smelling of cologne.

"So how'd you get into this? Weed? Theft?"

"Sort of." I add, "Taylor told me I could get a job, maybe. Career-wise."

"He said that?" Tareq's eyes have a mocking shine. "He told you his name is Taylor?"

"Says he got it from his Italian side. He told me all about it."

"That's a good story."

Now I'm angry. Tareq wasn't there when me and Taylor shot hoops. Or talked. Taylor wouldn't lie to me.

"Lemme see."

"What?"

Impatient, he says, "The wire."

I yank up my shirt and show him.

212

"Nice. No more than a pimple, huh?" He points. "Try not to bend or you'll muffle the sound. Always face him when you're talking."

I stuff my shirt back into my waistband. "How long have you done this?" I venture as we back down the driveway.

"Don't ask."

"But—"

Suddenly the car lurches to a stop. He twists around. His eyes flare. "No questions about me. Got it?"

I nod, scared.

Then he laughs, the way I've seen before, easing us onto the street. His voice has softened. "Come on, Naeem, lighten up. This is dope. We'll have fun. You'll see."

And we're off in the Batmobile. A cool thrill cuts through my veins. My pulse quickens. This is it. Driving on a cloud of fumes, out and up the BQE ramp. The seat holds me like a cloud. I'm on a mission. On my way.

A stillness draws around us when we pull up to the street opposite Ibrahim's apartment. Tareq settles back to gaze at the driveway, rubbing his temples. Nothing stirs. The street is glossy with heat. Even the drainpipes, the metal mail-boxes on the houses, are tipped in honey light.

Tareq's seat creaks as he turns to me. The sockets of his eyes are punch-tired. "Listen. If you do get him to come in the car, make sure he sits in the front."

"Why?"

He smacks the dashboard. "Camera."

213

"Wow."

I still can't believe this is really happening. A wire taped to my waist? A camera in the dashboard? Is he *serious*? The crazy thing is the person I most want to tell is Ibrahim. Instead I'm in an alternative universe, sitting next to Tareq, only it isn't really Tareq. It's some guy in a dry-cleaned shirt, cuffs folded just so.

"I don't understand," I say. "Why do you even need me?" I point to the dashboard. "You've got a camera. You can wear a wire."

"He trusts you. What am I supposed to do, just walk up and knock on his door?"

"I guess not." I stare out at the house. The blinds are drawn on the top floor. Looks like no one else is home. Maybe even Ibrahim isn't there. "How long does it take?"

He shrugs. "Hard to tell."

"What if—" I hesitate. "What if it's nothing?"

"Then we'll know."

I consider this. "And how long do I have to be involved?"

He grins. "Sick of me already?"

"No—"

He punches me in the arm. "Just kidding, man. Seriously. You're the conduit. The joint connecting us all. You're the one who'll keep Ibrahim's guard down. Without you, an operation like this could take months and months. Waste of time, waste of resources. You are gold, man."

So I am important. A crucial link.

He smacks the dashboard again. "Okay. Showtime."

CHAPTER 25

THE THING ABOUT SUPERHEROES IS IT'S ALL ABOUT LAYERS, SHADows. All the bad guys—Two-Face, the Joker—they once were good. They wore skins of light. They walked on pavement like the rest of us. Then something knifed them, deep. You never know. That's what Taylor's shown me. How to find the dark pain slipping out from under the skin. Growing like serpents in unwashed hair.

Who was Ibrahim to me? A liar? A lone wolf? What did I know? Maybe I didn't see the dark edge around his mouth, his eyes. Maybe we were moving too fast for me to notice. Underground all along.

My knees are shaking as I walk up the driveway. The wire feels thick against my waist, gives a little burn where the tape pinches. Tareq's car remains parked. I see his hand

215

in the rearview mirror, hanging. He flicks a cigarette butt to the ground.

"Ibrahim?"

I rap softly on the door at first. No one is out. The yards are still. Plastic bags are swept up stiff against the fence.

"Ibrahim!"

There's a shuffling inside, then a pause. "Who's there?"

"It's me. Naeem."

"I'm busy, man."

"I wanna talk to you. Want you to meet someone."

There's a slide and clack of a dead bolt drawing back. Ibrahim's narrow face peers through the crack.

"Who?"

"A friend."

He withdraws into the corridor, leaving the door ajar. He's wearing a pair of women's slippers that flap against his heels. When we enter the small apartment, I notice several spiral notebooks left open on the table. Scribbles in tiny, meticulous lettering.

"You working?"

"I told you. I have stuff to do."

"Awesome. Maybe I can help."

He turns and scrutinizes me. My heart gallops into my mouth. *It's blown. He knows.*

He says, "Serendipity. You know what that means?"

"Chance?"

"That's right. *Ser-en-di-pi-ty.*" He draws the word out. "Connections. Chance. There are bigger chances out there.

Bigger than getting through some three-credit class, you know?"

"That's what I mean. I have some leads."

"Yeah?"

"A guy. He knows how to do things. He can hook you up. Help you make your plans real." Even as I say it I feel like my words make no sense. What if his plans are nothing? Just his usual schemes?

"Who?"

"I told you! This guy. Tareq. I know him. He's cool."

"Where is he?"

I gesture to the door. "Outside."

He looks confused. He runs his hand through his hair. "Does he know about me?"

I stare at him, not understanding.

"I have ideas, you know. Not just one. People know."

This is weird. For a brief second I'm reminded of Zahir and his fever dreams.

"You wanna come?" I try again.

He hesitates. I can see the decision working away inside him. Then he takes off the slippers and puts on his sneakers. As we leave the house, I feel as if I'm taking some kind of pale-skinned creature from water into land, air. His neck cranes. He half hobbles to the car, eager.

"Ibrahim!" Tareq grins. His teeth shine in the sunlight. "Heard so much about you, man."

Ibrahim's gaze narrows. "Like what?"

"Only good stuff."

There's a hunger in Ibrahim's eyes as he takes in the car. The nice hubcaps, Tareq's arm draped over the door, showing his watch with tiny diamonds studded around the face.

"This your car?" Ibrahim touches the hood.

"It is. I have another car, a Benz. But it's in the shop."

"That must cost a lot."

"I have people who give me what I need."

"The watch too?"

"Yes. A present."

There's a hesitation. Tareq taps his middle-finger ring on the half-open window. "Ride?"

Ibrahim's head wobbles yes.

And then we're in.

I watch it.

The whole mesmerizing show. A slow-motion reel of what Ibrahim did in Macy's, with his posh accent and story about graduation. But better. Tareq, with his barrel chest, a gold chain buried in chest hair, is boastful, but not too much. Ibrahim's fingers feather around the radio settings. The car's got surround sound, a screen that slides down in the back, heated seats. Ibrahim checks it all out.

"You like nice things?" Tareq asks.

"Oh yeah."

"I can see that about you. What model you partial to?"

"I had my eye on a 640i Gran Coupe."

"They're not bad. Good engine."

"The Coupe's a waste. Not that different."

Tareq laughs. "Don't get too caught up in that stuff. We gotta keep our eyes on the real road. Right?"

Ibrahim nods vigorously. "Right."

We drive down Hillside Avenue, passing redbrick apartment buildings, a park of yellowed grass. The day gleams. I sink back in the soft seats, listen. It's beautiful, what Tareq does. He never says jihad right out. Not even Islam. But I can hear the thin whisper of line reeling in. How cars are good but we have to remember who we are. What matters. How we brothers have to stick together. Keep on the path. I couldn't have dreamed up a better ruse. Ibrahim getting dished to him just the way he did to the Macy's salesman! To me! I want to laugh.

We talk and talk, stopping only to buy ourselves cold fruit shakes from a Mexican cart. The ice and seeds crunch cold against our teeth. Tareq fussily blots a spill on the upholstery with paper napkins, like a grandmother. He's smooth, but hovering too, a cousin, an uncle, concerned. *What's that little scratch on your face, Ibrahim? You want me to get some ointment? You know, you remind me of my little cousin Amir.*

As we're off again, Tareq cocks a smile. "There are people I know, Ibrahim, who would be very interested in a guy like you. You're smart, you're quick, I can see that. We could work something out."

Ibrahim's head bobs a few times, as if on a spring. "I have ideas." His pale neck looks so skinny, I want to put my hand there, cover him.

Tareq tosses over his shoulder. "Isn't that right, Naeem?"

"Yeah, sure." My voice is thick in my throat. "Ibrahim, he always—"

"He's a leader," Tareq interrupts. "That's obvious. Not like this joker back here." He jabs a thumb at me. Ibrahim laughs.

I hunch down, smoldering, and catch Tareq's eyes in the rearview mirror, signaling *Play along.*

At the end of the day, we have a meal in Little Guyana on Liberty Avenue, where they serve curry chicken and thick rotis that drape over our fingers, leave grease spots on our paper plates. When we get in the car again, groggy and full, I start to get a little sick. Like with Taylor, driving lulls. The streets unfold. Buildings shimmer, fall back behind. Once in a while the skyline of Manhattan staggers up on the horizon. In this car we're different. I'm not that kid you see running down the block, knapsack bouncing on his back, terrified he's going to miss his train. I'm better than him. It's like a drug, this driving.

Anything's possible.

CHAPTER 26

THROUGH THE LONG LATE-AUGUST AND EARLY-SEPTEMBER weeks, we're wading deep into our work on Ibrahim.

Summer doesn't want to end; the heat's a clenched fist that won't release. Zahir is marching off to fifth grade, a big year, when he has to test for the middle schools. Abba and Amma have agreed he should try for the competitive ones, out of the neighborhood. I finished my English class. Got a B–. Not bad for someone who couldn't scrape by before.

My parents' store continues to do better. There was a big rush around the start of school—one afternoon mothers and kids were jostling into each other in the narrow aisle. We sold out of pencils and pocket folders. Amma has decided to stock notebooks and pen cases. *The girls like these,* she says, showing me the ones with shiny purple flowers.

And I am always moving, always in the cushioned ride of Tareq's car. When I shut my eyes, I see the city rolling smoothly beneath me. The neighborhoods, the boroughs, a quilted dream. This is better than Zahir's comic books, better than any ruse Ibrahim and I could make up. It's easy, being with Tareq. I get used to the heavy curve of his shoulders, the way he handles a stick shift. He's in charge, tough, and I like that. We drive, we talk. I confess to him how I've never been good at anything, really. Never made it to the finish line. "Yeah," he agrees. "Feels good to get stuff *done.*"

After a couple of weeks, I stop wearing the wire. No need. We have the dashboard cam.

Every other day, we go to see Ibrahim. Even without the wire, Tareq tells me I'm still the link, what keeps him softening to us. "Can't do it without you, man." In the meantime Tareq brings gifts: samosas, plump with potatoes and peas; a cotton jacket; a new backpack. Ibrahim's working a few shifts at the gas station. Somehow they took him back. But that seems to worsen his state. He meets us after his shift, changes in the backseat, clawing off his greasy clothes. It pains me to see him so famished for a new life, a new skin.

Cultivation. A slow unspooling.

Tareq gently presses Ibrahim's take on Islam. At first Ibrahim is evasive. He goes on a few sites, yes. His eyes flash to me, as if for approval. "You too, Naeem?"

"Yeah. Sometimes." The lie sits in my throat.

"Those guys are wild! They have ideas."

"Yeah."

"See what I mean? Forget about school. This is boss."

I don't answer. I never say a word about my new math class, or doing well. I don't want to set him off. Besides, it's the same as the old days—a flash of boasting, then a withdrawal. No new schemes, but Ibrahim admits there's some guy in England he's been emailing with. "Do you ever think about leaving?" Tareq asks.

"Yes," Ibrahim replies. "But there's work I can do here, right?"

I see the slight movement in Tareq. "That's why I'm here, *bhayia*." He smiles. Brother.

The hook is in.

By mid-October we're in rich waters. Tareq explains he has connections. A friend who has *stuff*. Ibrahim's left eye twitches. "I don't know," he mumbles. He looks a little scared, but excited too. Tareq keeps at it. Slow pressure, moving us further, into darker patches, seeing if Ibrahim follows. At first hesitant, Ibrahim turns to me. "What do you think?" he asks worriedly.

"It's cool."

"You in?"

I pause, then remember: It's like acting. Just do it. "Sure."

He looks assured, as if he needs us to make the talk

real. I can't believe I'm doing this, but after in the car, with Ibrahim gone, Tareq even compliments me. "That was beautiful. You're my closer, man."

"Yeah." I'm smiling too hard, my cheek muscles stiff.

"Seriously. You've got staying power. You're good at this."

But the next day, the more we drive, the queasier I get in the backseat. Tareq's patter has started up again, a little more urgent. When do we stop? When does Tareq pull the car to the curb and we three can lean against the car doors, our sides split with laughter? Call the whole thing a joke? But no, we're on Queens Boulevard. Tareq is talking about targets. I don't even remember how we got to this.

"You serious?" Ibrahim asks.

"Just hypothetical," Tareq assures him. To my relief, he drops it.

A few days later, though, he starts up again. A nudge forward, quiet, to see if Ibrahim is following. *Aaste dar ta-ano, jal beshi nareeyo na.* Row gently. Don't stir the water.

"If you were to do something big, where would it be? New York?" Tareq asks.

"Gotta be. Center of everything," Ibrahim answers.

Are they talking about what I think they're talking about?

"But how?"

"There are ways."

"With what?" Ibrahim asks.

"I have to talk to my guys. See what they can do." He checks his watch. "You hungry, *bhayia*?"

This is what Tareq always does. He lures, then stops. Offers a meal. It makes Ibrahim feel cared for, rewarded, fed. *The fish is hungry.*

Ibrahim and I watch Tareq hitch up his pants around his waist, head into a pizza parlor to get us some slices that we'll eat in the car. He does that a lot, so all our conversations can be recorded. Ibrahim and I are left alone, which doesn't happen much. I know the dashboard camera is switched off. Anything we say now is off the record.

"Hey, Ibrahim," I ask. "You really down with this?"

He looks at me, puzzled.

"It's kind of weird," I go on. "I mean, a few months ago, you were into stuff. Like the suit—"

"That was before," he says dreamily.

"Before what?"

"Before I met Tareq-bhayia."

I'm starting to panic. If it weren't for me, there wouldn't be a Tareq. He wouldn't be here, hanging on his every word.

Stop, I want to signal to Ibrahim. *Stop.*

Shadows drape over the windshield. I'm in the front seat now. The camera switched off. Tareq and I listen to the slow tick-tick of the engine, just turned off, sighing through the cylinders.

Ibrahim is maneuvering down the driveway, past the bulky SUV. He's excited like a kid just back from his first day of school. I'm starting to understand the shape of this plan. He hasn't said it out loud yet, but I can see it, like stones leading out of dark water to a shore, shining ahead. Equipment. Targets. Some kind of pretend operation.

"Not bad for a few months' work," Tareq comments. "That guy, man, was ready. Never seen anything like it."

I stare down at my hands, which look thin and bony. "I don't know. I never heard Ibrahim talk this way. You're the one who's pushing him. Like that talk about targets. He'd never think that up."

He slides his sunglasses over his head, massages his eyes. "Don't get philosophical on me, man."

"You've done this awhile," I venture.

This time he doesn't cut me off. "Yeah," he sighs. "They put me on a lot of assignments."

"That's cool."

His voice is low. "Yeah. Right."

A twilight-sad feeling draws down through me. I remember the rumors: How Tareq was supposed to go to prison. But then that evaporated. Now Tareq seems about a hundred years old, older than Abba, even.

I ask timidly, "After this . . . what happens to you?"

He shrugs. "Texas, maybe. Chicago. You do this for a while, people start to figure out who you are. It's better if they keep you moving. Places where they don't know you."

"Don't you ever want to stop?"

He turns toward me. His eyes are deep, tired. "Naeem. I can't stop. This is all I have."

And then it really hits me: if he wasn't in this corner, it would be another one, far worse. Prison. Why did I think it was anything else?

"Give it two days," he says. "That way, he gets a chance to get worked up. Okay?"

"Okay."

Outside, yellow leaves scuttle at my feet. I cut across a park, moving in and out of patches of chilled air and sun. I remember on the grass with the kids this summer. Their eager, sometimes angry talk. How much I liked it. I didn't really even say good-bye to them once the camp ended. By that time I was in too deep with Tareq.

I'm not sure where I want to go now: Back to the store? Home? I've got two pages of equations. Maybe I can duck into a coffee shop, shake my sadness. For the first time, I know: I've lost my friend.

When I get to the apartment, I find Zahir sitting cross-legged on his bed. The comic books, all the ones I've bought him, have been put away. The Spider-Man towel is gone. "Hey," I ask. "What happened to your stuff?"

He turns, a serious look on his face. "You know, I've been thinking. I'm not so into Spider-Man. I think my favorite superhero is Batman."

"Why?"

He cups his chin in his hands, considers. "Because he raised himself to be a genius. He's the smartest superhero. He doesn't have any special powers." He tilts his head and gives me a sly look. "And he's a billionaire."

Laughing, I rumple his hair. "How's that math going?"

As I'm leaving the bedroom, I notice there are two

227

missed calls on my cell phone, from a number I don't recognize. No message. I hit Call Back.

"Naeem?" The voice is high, a woman's, rushing in.

"Yeah?"

"My name is Mrs. Syed. Shirin is my given name. You
are friend of Ibrahim's?"

"Yes," I say slowly.

I can hear the relief on the other side. "Please. I am
worried about my boy. Can you come see me?"

CHAPTER 27

IBRAHIM'S MOTHER IS YOUNGER THAN I EXPECTED. SORT OF LIKE my stepmother, but her face is long, resembling Ibrahim's, and deeply scored with lines. She lets the three bolt locks snap back before she swings the door open. I see a small apartment with the nylon curtains drawn. Not that much different from the apartment where I found Ibrahim.

"Come in, come in!"

I chuck off my shoes and follow her down a narrow hall. We sit at a table, where she sets down a plate of dry biscuits. "Please, eat."

"No, thank you, Auntie." It's hard for me to even look at her. I try to sit angled away from her. Just a few minutes. Then I'll be on my way.

"You want Nescafé?"

"That's okay."

Since I don't speak Urdu, we talk in English, but it's a struggle for her. I feel bad, seeing how she pushes the words out, halting, slow. "I am so very glad to meet you," she says. "He is always saying Naeem this, Naeem that!"

"Really?" A tiny glow opens in me.

When she smiles, she has a gap between her two front teeth. "I say all the time, bring him home, bring him home! But he tells me you are so busy with school."

"I guess."

She keeps fiddling with her head scarf. "I find your number in his old phone." She adds, "You have seen him?"

Here I grow uneasy. "Yes," I say carefully. I glance around for signs of Ibrahim. On one wall, over a cabinet, several photos are arrayed, but I don't see any of him.

"I am worried," she says. "He calls me last night. He says many things I don't understand. So much, I do not know what he does now. He is not living with us. He stays at apartment of relative who is away. He is leaving when my husband gets angry. My husband is working very hard."

"His taxis?" I ask.

"Taxis?" She looks puzzled.

"Ibrahim said your husband has a bunch of taxis? He drove me in one once."

An uncertain look flashes across her face. "There are no taxis," she sighs. "Once, little time, my husband work for taxi company."

"So he doesn't own one?"

"No!" She is surprised. "You know how much medallion cost?"

I nod. Of course I know. I never believed the business about the fleet, but I thought maybe one car. But this apartment is cramped. The table we're sitting at is so small our knees nearly touch. The sofa is stacked with blankets. There's only one bedroom, probably for the kids. The parents sleep in the living room. Why did I think otherwise?

"So . . . ," I say slowly. "Why did Ibrahim leave?"

"He has fight with my husband."

I notice she never calls him Ibrahim's father. She goes on, shaking her head.

"We come here and my husband is driving taxi. Then he gets job. He works for man on Long Island. Good job, very good job! Private driver. Jewish man. Very nice man.

"Sometimes Ibrahim goes with my husband to work. He stay at house while my husband drive employer all around. He say, okay, I clean cars or do something for you. Man is very nice to Ibrahim. Tell him things. You do this. Do that. You study, go to college. He give him money, even, go buy books for school."

She gets up from the table and lifts up a picture that's been snuck into another frame. There he is: in aviator sunglasses, leaning against the hood of a green Mercedes-Benz, thumbs up. A big sand-colored house with hedges in the background.

She shakes her head. "Then Ibrahim do bad things."

"Like?"

She glances away. "He goes into man's wife's bathroom. Use her bath."

I can't help myself: a tickle of laughter pushes up in

231

my throat. I can imagine crazy Ibrahim, padding around in some rich lady's bathroom, testing the taps, tipping bottles of fancy bubble bath into the swirling water.

"That's not so bad—"

Her voice goes hushed. "Then he start to take things. Maybe watch here. Clothing. Shirt. Sometimes he takes out car! First they have no idea. One time he use credit card. Go to big restaurant. Even hotel, sign in as my husband's boss! They find out and very big problem. My husband, he realize. He get very angry. They have big fight. 'You are liar and thief!' He kick him out of house." She starts to rub her face, several times. "We do not do this. We do not send a boy to street."

I let out a thin stream of air. "Wow. That must be hard. To kick out your own son."

Her neck jerks up, as if on a spring. "Ibrahim never tells you?"

"Tells me what?"

She hesitates. "He is not my son."

"I don't understand. Ibrahim's dad—"

She says softly, "Ibrahim. He is nobody's son."

"What?"

"We take him in many years ago. Cousin of my husband. They are very poor and they are having trouble. Nobody want him. My husband has big heart. So we take him as favor. But this time when they start to fight, my husband he say very bad things. He says Ibrahim is his shame. Nobody's boy."

She sucks in her breath. This time I look at her full on to see the pain.

"I think . . ." She is searching for the word. "I think this breaks him."

That word—*break*—sits between us. The air goes quiet.

Now I understand the pictures. In a gold frame is a big wedding photo—what looks like a younger Shirin, still bony and narrow-faced, and a plump man, sitting stiffly in front of pillows, his embroidered turban sitting a little crooked on his head. I can imagine what she says: *My husband has big heart.* He looks outgoing, the one who pushes himself into a knot of men, makes them laugh. Then several pictures of two boys, twins, in front of matching green bicycles, or waving. They look round-faced, like their father, belonging. But none of Ibrahim. As if he doesn't exist.

"Ibrahim call me last night, late. He is talking fast, very fast. I cannot follow. He is saying all kind of crazy things. Big plan, he tell me. He is going to do good. He say he meet some man."

I sit up, alert. "A man?"

"Yes. I think, this makes no sense. Anyone, they offer you money like that, it's no good. But then he say, this man. He knows you?" Her gaze turns to me, imploring.

I try to swallow, but there's a dry catch in my throat. "Yes."

"That's why I call you. I think, Naeem, he is good boy. In school. He is Ibrahim's friend. He can tell me."

I feel as if my head is filling with bits of sharp metal. I will never be able to get up from this table, never be able to speak. What do I say? "I know this man," I say slowly.

She smiles. Her eyes shine with relief. "I knew it."

Her stockinged feet give a little whisper as she rises. She clutches my arm. "Ibrahim, he is always like this. Love big talk. Money. He is kind of boy, he gets . . ." She struggles again with the word. "Easy trust. Impressed." She smiles. "My English is not so good."

I say gently, "No, Auntie, it's very good."

She sighs. "I am not happy he leaves the family. But my husband says, a boy, he has to go away to find himself." She adds, hopeful, "You will speak to him? No matter my husband says. I treat him like my own."

"Yes, yes." Then I add, "I'll take care of it."

"Thank you."

We move toward the door and I put my shoes back on.

"Inshallah, it will be better," she says.

"Inshallah, it will, Auntie."

And I slip out the door.

CHAPTER 28

DOORS.

Doors that I pushed open when I was five years old. I was searching for my amma, for some part of myself that was torn away. That is what my father explained: when someone dies, they take a piece of you.

Doors. Abba told me how the soldiers knocked on his family's door, during the time when his brother Rasul disappeared to the Freedom Fighters. They knifed the pillows, feathers scattering. They snapped open the lock on the cupboard and pulled out saris and chiffons and cottons, laughing. Abba saw how his parents suffered. He became the cautious one. The clutch of fear showed in his eyes. He could not trust. He did not want courage. He left for America to not be so afraid anymore. But the fear didn't go away. There are always new doors, here too.

As I make my way to meet Tareq a few blocks from Ibrahim's apartment, I close my eyes and I see how it will happen for Ibrahim. Knuckles on wood. Badges flicked from a jacket pocket. Men in dark blue Windbreakers shoulder in. The woman staring on the other side of the fence, her mouth a surprised O.

You read about it in the papers or on TV. The kind of news that makes your parents tuck their necks in just a little more. But now I know. It's a door that's been put there. And my friend is going to walk right through it.

I walk until I can't stand it anymore and I stop by the side of the pavement and throw up into the hedges. I wipe the sourness away with the back of my hand, dry my fingers in the stiff leaves. When I turn, I see Tareq's shadow in the shiny BMW.

"You're late," Tareq says. He flicks his wrist, showing the fancy watch. His eyebrows gather to a bushy dark point. "That's not good."

"Sorry. I had to help my father." The passenger seat creaks as I slide in beside him. "Listen. Can we talk?"

"About?"

"This. The plan."

He shakes his head. "We went over it a million times. Just get him in the car. That's all. I'll take care of the rest." He inserts the key in the ignition.

Desperate, I grab his arm. "Wait. Tareq. I don't know about this—"

He gives me a cross-eyed, puzzled look. "What are you talking about?"

My hands are fisted in my lap. "I saw his mother. I mean, she's not his real mother, but she raised him. She called me. Ibrahim's kind of mixed up." I don't like the sound of my voice—pleading.

He scowls. "Naeem, we have a plan."

"I know." And then it rushes out of me. "They said it's a conveyor belt, right? Why can't he just get off? We can go in there. Tell him he's in trouble. We can take him over to Taslima's group. Or Mahmoud's. They can talk to him—"

Furious, Tareq leans in, grabs my shirt, breathing heavily. "Are you out of your mind?"

I stare at him.

"This isn't a little game, Naeem. *Tell* him?"

"Not everything—"

He lets go of my shirt. My throat throbs.

"I knew it," he says, shaking his head. "They should have never brought you in. Punk."

No! I want to say, but my mouth's sealed shut.

Tareq turns on the car and we drive toward Ibrahim's. My whole body is braced against the seat. As if trying to slow us down. One block, two. Ibrahim's street. We park, and he shuts off the ignition. The house is still. Everything's still. Silence against my ears. His thumb is stroking the steering wheel. His voice is low. "I don't think you get it, Naeem. I'm not going to let you screw this up."

"Why not?" I hate how thin and whiny my voice is.

He sighs. "In this whole scheme, you're nothing. I'm

nothing. We're vermin. Mice. Chasing crumbs. And I'm sure as hell not going to let you take me off the chase. You hear?"

"Yes."

Tareq snatches the keys into his palm. "You get your act together, you hear?" When I don't move, he scowls. "You coming?"

I don't answer.

"Naeem?"

The engine's ticking is up my throat, through my mouth, sighing through the cylinders.

"Come on, man, you're my closer." He tries a fist bump but I don't go for it.

The next thing I knew I'm slammed hard against the door. My shoulder spikes with pain. Tareq's face is tight against mine, his voice ragged-angry. "Naeem. If you're not there, he gets nervous. You know that."

I can't stand it. The nausea wells up in me. I tear off my seat belt and fling open the door.

"Yo!" I hear behind me.

But I don't stop. The heat smacks me in the face. For an instant, I weave on the pavement. But then I'm running, running, I don't know where.

CHAPTER 29

GOTHAM, MY GOTHAM.

I remember when Abba sent me those postcards, back in Bangladesh. The Empire State Building. Yankee Stadium. A night skyline of Manhattan, black ink and diamonds. I could not believe I would live in such a place. That it might be mine. My abba, the man who scuffed down the hall each morning in his faded, checked lungi and T-shirt, set his rough hand on my cheek, had disappeared into its magic canyons. But it was true. And he sent for me too. He believed we had found a magic place without fear. Never again would he be as afraid as he'd been in his own home.

And now I am running through the city I found. All I know is I have to move, to keep going. If I run, no one will know. That I was part of the plan, the story, the door that opened the other way. All I know is I can't be there, not in that corner. Not what Tareq is.

Past the high school where I once kissed a girl, Sheena. I would wait at the bottom of the stairs, every molecule in my body wanting her. But she's evaporated. Why was she so important? My stupid teenage years, every cut class, every mistake zooms past me.

Then I'm on the subway stairs, on a train. The stops slide past. My breaths are even now; the sweat pricks dry on my skin. At the Union Turnpike stop, more people stream in. It's the end of the day. I don't want to go home yet. I can't.

I get out at the Woodhaven Boulevard stop and walk up Queens Boulevard, traffic moving thick as syrup. My phone buzzes in my pocket. Tareq. A text. *Call me.* I delete it. Then another. *Okay, you had your little freak out. Time to come back. Bhayia?* Now a voice message: *Come on, man. This is your chance. Carry through for a change.* This one stung. Then a string of texts from Taylor, cooler, not letting on. *Just checking in, buddy. Everything OK? See u today? What's up? Talk? Check in?*

I delete them all, walk fast down Ninetieth Street toward the neighborhood I know so well. Up ahead, rising above all the low little houses, is my high school. When I first saw the place it looked like a fairy-tale castle. Turrets, funny-shaped windows, an arched front door. I was sure once I stepped inside it would be magic. I'd change, miraculously, from that middle school kid who'd screwed up. I'd turn back to good.

The school is closed, of course. Not even the security guard I used to sneak past. For a second I see a light on behind a window blind and my heart gives a little jump. I think about Mrs. D, sitting behind her piles of folders, chiding me. What would she think of what I'm doing?

Maybe there aren't miracles anymore.

The Q53 is just pulling into the stop on Woodhaven Boulevard. Before I know it, I'm springing up the steps and sitting in the back. The bus engine rumbles and groans. I lean against the cool window, shut my eyes.

It must be an hour later when I finally get out at the beach. I smell of diesel and my shirt is crumpled. In the window I can see my hair stands up on end. Outside, there's a woman selling mangos on a stick, cut up in a long flower shape, sprinkled with salt. I buy one, sucking down the sweet shreds as I make my way to the boardwalk.

It's still not dark. Joggers pass, weaving between mothers with their strollers. A pair of old ladies in matching pink tracksuits power-walk, elbows scissoring at their sides. The air is crumbling, falling into the gray sea as pink-blue dust. I can see, on the slowly emptying beach, a guy in a uniform stabbing garbage from the sand with a long pole. I kick off my sneakers and head down.

The instant I hit sand the temperature lowers. A breeze cuts in and sweeps up from below, grazes my bare ankles. Everything smells briny-wet. I roll up my jeans, push my way across the sand toward the water.

Slowly, I inch my way in, feet sinking into the shallows. First my ankles, then all the way to my knees. The bottom of my pants tug heavy, but I don't care. I bend, washing off the grit of the city, this day. As if I haven't washed in a thousand days.

Then I go over to a jetty, where I sit for a while, watching the wavelets slap up against greasy rock. What is my family doing now? I picture Zahir coming off the bus a few hours ago. Eating his ices, sitting on the stool in the shop, bending the paper cup so he gets every last drop. His tongue streaked blue. Then Amma takes him back to the apartment to make supper, while Abba stays back in the shop. I know the routine: counting the bills for the cash bag, turning out lights, the last bundle of cardboard for the curb, snapping off the Xerox machine. By now a patch of black sky shows through the rear window. By now they are checking how many hours in the stretch between prayer and food and sleep and waking. This is their duty, their home.

What's mine?

Waves sigh. The night is full on now, cold, even. I can't make out my legs against the stone. The line between shore and water dims and blurs. There are lights winking on at my back. Stores, houses, apartments, people going on to the next chore, the next moment. I sit. I'm so tired. I'm ancient-sea-creature tired. A million years have passed this summer and fall. A million tiny bones broken. I'm just a fish, a scale, powder. Nothing.

So many times this summer, Abba said: *We need to take the day off. Go to the beach. I can fish. You boys can swim.* But it never happened. We never unlatched the links of our days to find ourselves.

I set my head on my arms and cry.

I made it here, Abba, I want to say. *I'm here.*

CHAPTER 30

Morning fog rolls in thickly across the beach. A horn bleats. It takes a moment for me to remember where I am. I texted my parents, told them I was sleeping at a friend's. They sounded worried, but after some back-and-forth, they gave in. So I spent the night under the boardwalk, managing to stay in the shadows so the cops didn't see. For some reason I felt safe. After all, I've been on their side, right? I wasn't afraid.

It wasn't an easy night: knees jammed against my chest, damp seeping up my haunches. I couldn't get warm. Now, sitting on a bench, I feel a fresh coolness stirring in the air. I buy two fried egg sandwiches and a muffin from a truck. I'm ravenous: I wolf everything down, watching the gulls caw and wheel across the sky.

I check my phone. More messages from Tareq. *I'll tell them. Everyone will know. How about that? Even your do-gooder Tas. Your girlfriend. You want that?* I remember Tareq tight up against me, the jagged pain in my shoulder. Then I swipe them all away.

It's still early. The bus is waiting by the corner; the driver finishing up a coffee before she tosses it into the garbage bin. It's the same bus I took to get here yesterday.

I pause, tilt my face up to the sky. It's Indian summer weather. A few trees are flush with burning color, as if ready to ignite: deep red, flame yellow. People are walking with their jackets folded over their arms, surprised by the sudden warmth. A surprise, a gift. I board the bus, take it back in the direction I came from.

A plastic jack-o'-lantern jeers on the top step of Ishrat's house. Clumps of cottony spiderweb are spread on the bushes.

The door opens. "What are you doing here?" she asks.

"Sorry."

She glances over her shoulder. She's thrown on a fluffy sweatshirt over her nightgown, used the hood to cover her hair. Her round face is still soft with sleep.

"Can we just sit here?" I point to the stoop.

"I guess."

Still in her bare feet, she steps out and sits down. I set-tle a few inches away from her. This is a quiet part of the neighborhood, just a distant chug and rattle of garbage trucks. We tip our chins up to the sun, soaking it in. It feels good. Not touching. Her shoulders near mine.

"You want some water or something?"

"No."

I don't explain myself. How can I? I got off the bus and walked and walked as a pink sky spread across the apartment roofs. Before I knew it I was in front of Ishrat's house, ringing the bell, lucky that she was the one to answer.

"We were wondering what happened to you," she says now. "You kind of disappeared at the end of camp. Didn't even say good-bye."

I don't answer.

"I was pissed," she goes on. "Really pissed."

I swivel to face her. It's funny how much she reminds me of Amma. The same little mole to the side of her mouth.

A woman pokes her head out the door. "Ishrat?"

"Hey, Ma."

Ishrat's mother looks so different from Ishrat. Her glossy black hair is cut at a fashionable slant, her face slender. I tense, thinking she's going to be upset to see me, but she just looks puzzled. "Oh, hello there!"

"Hi." I give a small, shy wave.

"This is Naeem. Remember I told you? From the camp?"

She brightens. "Why are you sitting there? Come in, come in, have some tea! You'll catch a cold." She speaks a British-accented English, educated.

"Ma," Ishrat laughs. "It's like *summer.*"

"Yes, I suppose that's so." She gives a small, impish smile.

Clearly she just wants to spy on us, get the scoop. I feel a stab of envy. How easy it seems for Ishrat, this choosing who she can be. Wearing a scarf. Sitting out on a stoop with a boy. The affectionate space between her and her mother.

"Good to meet you, Naeem," her mother says as she lets the screen door flap shut. "Come see us again! You're always welcome!" she sings out. I can imagine her just as Ishrat described: doing theater, smoking cigarettes with her university friends.

It's time to go. I don't want to. But I feel it.

I rise from the steps and say, "You're going to hear things about me."

Her eyes seem to lighten. She says nothing.

"They're true."

She spreads her broad hands across her knees. "Okay."

"Okay-okay?" I ask.

"Yes," she laughs.

I start to walk down the path. "See you," she calls.

I turn once. Her nightgown drapes over her legs. But I can just see the jutting bones of her ankles. For some reason, this makes me happy. "Yeah." I smile. "See you around."

From all the way down the corridor, I can hear her jangling keys. I jump up from the floor. Taslima's moving toward me, backpack slung over her shoulder. Her hair is freshly washed, damp-wet around her neck. She stops, her eyes opening with surprise.

"Well, well. Long time no see." She's angry.

247

I shrug. "Yeah."

"You look terrible."

"I'm okay."

"Are you?"

"No," I admit.

Setting her hands on her hips, she gives me the once-over: my rumpled jeans, my unwashed hair and face. I can tell she isn't sure whether to be pissed or worried about me. "What's going on?" I know what she really wants to ask: *Where the heck have you been these past weeks?* But she manages to hold herself back.

"Can we go inside?"

"You have a problem?"

"Not like you think."

Wary, she unlocks the door, flips on the light switch. The room floods with a pale fluorescence that hurts my eyes.

Taslima waits for a cue from me. But I don't know where to begin. I decide to drag out two metal folding chairs, the way we do for group talk. This time a circle of two. She sits across from me, picking at her fingernails. I'm aware of the sand shaking out of my jeans every time I shift on the chair. My shirt feels greasy and my teeth have a funky film.

"So you know how I came to you this summer? Looking for work?"

"Yeah. I did it for Uncle. To keep you out of trouble."

I nod. "I was already in trouble."

She tilts her head, puzzled.

248

"I got caught . . . with some stolen stuff. Shirts. Then some weed . . ." My voice trails off.

"Uncle knows this?"

"My parents don't know anything."

"But how—how could they not know? I mean—don't you have a court date or something?"

I can't speak. I lean my palms on either side of my thighs, on the cold metal, as if to eject the words.

"I made a deal."

"A deal?"

"I got a job. Kind of like an assignment." I add, "For the cops."

It takes a minute. Her shoulders jerk back, as if she's been struck. "You? This whole—"

"The whole time," I admit.

"The kids? The camp—"

"All of it."

Taslima drops her head, elbows on her knees, the thin wings of her shoulder blades drawn tight. She looks like she's going to be sick. Then she hurls her backpack, straps fluttering, against a wall. Calls me every kind of curse and name, in Bangla and English. But I stay with it, with her. Even when she tells me to go and then takes it back, I don't slink away. I've never done that before.

"How could you do this?"

My thoughts are swimming. "I don't know! It's not so bad."

"Not so bad! You think you're doing some *good*?"

"Yes!" I say hotly. "I was trying to protect you. Others. Help. These are kids! People. Lots of people." I bite down on what I want to say: *guys like Ibrahim.* But I can't tell her. "It happens, Taslima, it does! Have you seen those videos? They're evil! They get sucked in! Like Noor!"

"What about her?"

"I told you! I didn't turn her in. I could have! I protected her! I protected all of you!"

"So you're proud of yourself?" she mutters.

"Yes! No."

"But to treat us all like criminals? Like would-be terrorists?" She spins around in the center of the room, slaps her sides. "Do you know how hard I work to build up trust with these kids? And you just kill it? Just like that?" She shakes her head. "I can't believe it. I can't."

"I'm sorry—"

"No, you're not!"

We stare at each other, breathing hard. Then I grab my backpack and rise. "Forget it. I shouldn't have come."

"You're right. You shouldn't have."

Outside it's started to rain, a metallic patter bouncing against the air-conditioning unit. Drops spatter the windows gray. I hunch, as if already protecting myself against the wet. I don't even know why I told her. This is the Taslima I've always known: righteous, so sure of herself. Why did I ever think she'd understand?

"Wait, Naeem." I turn. "Why did you come here?"

I run my tongue over dry lips. I feel as if my whole body is loosening, breaking apart. "I want out," I breathe.

Taslima's shoulders go soft. "Of course," she whispers. "Of course you do."

She throws me a weary smile. She looks tired. I am too, a deep and long exhaustion, like being creased and folded in too many times. All of us are. I wish we could live in another time, when we could have a camp and paint murals and kick a soccer ball. That's all we want. All everyone wants. To be normal.

Now she fetches her backpack from across the room, scoops up her car keys. "Let's go."

"Where?"

"Tim. My ex-husband," she explains. "He runs a law clinic."

I hesitate. "You don't have to do that."

"I know."

Taslima snaps off the light. We stand for a brief moment in the dark. I can feel her draw near me, smell the musk of her hair, sandalwood on her skin. She puts her arms around me. There are just her skinny arms, her flinty elbows. So much air and space between us.

"Oh, you stupid, stupid boy," she murmurs.

CHAPTER 31

I WALK TOWARD TAYLOR.

It's still morning. The burst of rain is gone, leaving the sky a smooth, polished blue. The streets seem rinsed and fresh, a damp, clean smell coming up from the ground. There's a smoke-crisp smell of fall in the air.

This is the same park where he and I first shot hoops, where the cops used to watch me, hidden behind tinted windshields. Scanning my knees, my ankles, my face. Who was I? Just some kid, maybe trouble, maybe not.

The same rubber-lined area where me and Jamal used to run into the spouting sprinklers. I laugh to think of that. We were just goofing. Not dirty or criminal. Not sure of what we were: monster or superhero or both.

Just kids. That's what Tim said to me: "You may be eighteen. But you're just a kid."

An hour ago, Taslima took me to Tim's apartment; he was there with a colleague. They were waiting for me.

When I walked in the door, my heart gave a jump. The pen guy. From my parents' shop! Tweed jacket, blowing on his coffee.

But when he stood to greet me, I saw I was wrong. He just looked like that guy. He held out his hand, warm, efficient. "Hi, I'm Salim. I work with Tim."

I already felt better. The three of us sat around Tim's dining table, going over my situation. I talked and watched as Salim's hand moved across a yellow legal pad. He tilted his head and listened. I felt as if I was being brought inside, into a new circle.

"The police don't have a hold on you," he finally explained. "None."

After months and months puffed up on lies, it was like someone had tugged on a cord, let all the pressure out of me. I wasn't a superhero. I was a cartoon float in some fake parade. I felt the hiss of air as I slowly drifted back to earth. I blinked. Everything felt hard but good too. Solid and hurting.

"That can't be. What about the weed, the shoplifting? My green card?"

Tim shook his head. "Not enough."

"But Tareq. He—" I hesitated. "He said he'd tell everyone."

Salim offers a sad smile. "He can't. It'll blow his cover too."

I thrust up from my chair. It took a few minutes to

process, rearrange the molecules in my body. "What do I do? I don't get it."

They told me not to answer any texts from Taylor or Tareq. Go dark on them. It was different with Taylor, I said. Tim admitted that these cops seemed to treat me a little better. Usually they rough guys up a lot more. But they both were firm on this point. *Never talk to a cop without your lawyer. You understand?* I thanked them over and over, put their card deep in my pocket, and left.

On the bus ride home, I kept hearing them: *You're not special, Naeem,* Salim and Tim kept saying. *Get that out of your head right now. They're using you.* Some part of me didn't believe it, didn't want to. And even though I knew it was stupid, I dug out my phone. Hit Taylor's number.

Meet me at the playground.

Now Taylor's striding toward me and my heart's jammed up in my throat. I'm surprised at how he looks like a kid himself, in high-top sneakers and a T-shirt. I wish I hadn't done this. He's a cop. I've never stood up to a cop before. No way. Tim and Salim were right. What am I doing here?

"Hey," I call.

"Hey." His body language is wary. "What's going on? Heard you cut out."

"I did." I look around the playground for Sanchez. Then I see him, one shoulder against a fence, near a bench.

"I need to talk to you."

Taylor is startled. I don't usually address him this way. "Sure."

We sit on the bench. I'm perched on a slat's edge. Taylor has his legs stretched out, hands cupped in his lap. I know him by now. Underneath he's nervous. We're tilted off the usual routine.

"I've been to see Ibrahim's mother. I mean, she's not exactly his mother—" I stop. "She called me."

I can feel Taylor tense. He sits up straight. "That right? You get spooked yesterday? That happens—"

"No," I interrupt. "I think—" It takes me a moment to find the words. "I think the only person Ibrahim wants to hurt is himself."

Taylor fastens those gray eyes on me. "They're the most dangerous kind, Naeem," he whispers.

I shiver, stay silent. A stray paper bag gusts up, droops down on the pavement.

"Naeem, a guy like that—"

"A guy like that?" I repeat. Like Tareq in the car, with nowhere to go? And Ibrahim?

I see him turning in those three-way mirrors, so many versions of himself, flashing back. *Nobody's son,* Shirin-Auntie had said. What happens when you put your hand through the mirror and there's nothing, just vapor? What do you reach for? A raw hurt swells up in my throat. "Low-lifes! That's who does this, right? What you thought I was?"

"Whoa, whoa, buddy. Slow down there."

"I'm out."

"What do you mean?"

"I'm not doing this anymore."

I see the flicker of anger, a tiny vibration. Sanchez is just a few feet away, ready to pounce. They can turn on me in a second. "Tareq is your friend, right? He had it all lined up. Months of work! And you're messing it up for him—"

"I know that."

He grimaces. "It doesn't work that way, Naeem. You can't just bail."

"Yes, I can."

"No way."

"That's bull!"

He flinches, as if a tiny whip cut his cheek.

I dig out Salim's card. "I've talked to my lawyer."

Taylor jerks up from the bench and smacks the fence. It rattles, shrill and metallic. Sanchez moves toward me, his face dark. I flinch, ready to fight. But Taylor puts up a warning hand. Then he returns to the bench and sits, kneading his fists between his knees. His shoulders slump. He looks old, so old. I never saw this before.

"Naeem. You've got this all wrong. It wasn't what you think. We actually like you. You have a future. We thought—I thought—you had something."

This time I'm not as afraid. He's grasping at air. Two-bit informer leads to a future, a career?

"I did have something," I say. "I do."

We sit in silence a while. I wait for him to tempt me. Another door. But it never comes.

"Is your name even Taylor?"

He turns, surprised. Then he looks away.

And that's when I know it's time to leave. I press my palms on the bench and rise. I feel light-headed. Taylor is still sitting, gazing at the playground. He looks contemplative.

"Hey," I say.

He lifts his head.

"Thank you."

He's confused. He has no idea why I'm thanking him.

Taylor isn't bad. He isn't good, either. I don't know what's good or bad anymore.

He just showed me. That I'm not such a screw-up. That I can do something. Do it all the way. On my own.

Abba that morning, standing in the kitchen. It is my choice, he said.

And maybe that's all courage is, I think. *Choosing.*

I head out of the park. And then I realize: that's the first time I've walked away from him.

CHAPTER 32

A THIN LIGHT SHOWS BENEATH THE DOOR CRACK.

I cringe. My parents must be furious. Turning the key, I slip inside, take off my sneakers, sand scattering softly to the mat. It's quiet and still in here. In the kitchen my amma is sitting at the table. Her head is bowed; I can see her slender neck, the careful part in her hair. My chest contracts. I'm sure she's crying. But no, she is just reading a prayer book, quietly, her lips moving. When she hears me, she startles. Even with her tired eyes, the scolding ready on her lips, she is joyous.

"Naeem," she says. "You're here."

"Yes, I am, Amma." I can't believe how glad I am to be home.

I slide into the chair opposite her. We don't talk. We don't have to. Midday glare is starting to seep through the

258

blinds. The faucet gives a *tap-tap*ping into the sink. Amma, I see, has set out the evening preparations—chopped onions, eggplant chunks already spotted brown, curry leaves curling up on the wooden board.

"You were not at your friend's," she says.

"No, I wasn't."

"I knew that." She kneads her temples, wisps of hair around her eyes. "Zahir showed me, on your computer."

I nod.

"You are in trouble?" she asks softly.

I'm sure my heart is going to break my rib cage. My parents never knew anything. My brushes with the law. The stupid pen and the calculator. My work with Taylor. None of it. I was a stranger among them, winged and secret. But maybe not. Maybe Amma always could see right into me, the shape of my hurt. I thought I was hidden, and I was not.

"No, Amma, it's okay."

"I did not think so." Her voice catches. "I read about boys getting in trouble in the paper. Mixed up in wrong things. They are not good."

"No, Amma. They're not."

There's a clatter of a garbage truck going by. Amma stirs up from the table, pulls out a plate of *luchis* that she puts in the microwave, and sets them down before me. They are warm, popping with moist heat. They melt against my teeth and tongue. I am ravenous. I did not know how much I needed this.

A faint buzzing, my phone, resting near my arm. A number flashing. Tareq, desperate. Wanting to meet. *Come* on, *Naeem. You're my closer. My bhayia.* I feel a pang. He is a brother and I've left him behind. If Ibrahim gets skittish on him, it's a lost gig. No money. Nothing. The whole sting could collapse.

The phone stills. Then it buzzes again, jumping a little on the table.

"Aren't you going to answer that?" she asks.

I shake my head. Then I look down at the remaining *luchis,* dimpled with steam. Once again I remember when I was so little, how I walked around our flat, pressing my palm to doors. *Amma, where are you?* I had cried. There were always more doors yawning open, out there, in me. This is what we all do: push a door, click on a site, and we don't know what chute we'll drop down.

But here, in this kitchen, the blinds glowing with sun, the door is open and this is what I find. Our rooms, Abba rising, pushing his callused feet into his slippers. Zahir swimming up from his dream-sea of numbers and dragons and superheroes, rubbing his eyes awake. A plate of *luchis* warm from the pan. They are around me. I am not alone.

Abba stands in the doorway, rumpled from sleep, his pajama bottoms wrinkled. It is Sunday, their one day off, and Amma always lets him sleep in. He has yet to do his prayers. I give him a cautious smile. He offers one. "You are back?"

Then I set my hand on Amma's. I can feel the atoms and molecules, life and connection, jumping through her veins. But I am looking at my father.

"Yes," I say. "Yes, I am."

AUTHOR'S NOTE

Though based on real issues and events, *Watched* is entirely a work of fiction.

I wrote this book while buffeted by painful headlines—the terrorist attacks in Paris, sting operations and further attacks in the United States, and the rise of ISIS and their slick recruitment of young people. My aim is to tell the human story behind the headlines, to explore the complicated choices and pressures teenagers—especially Muslim teenagers—face when their world is so riven and made precarious by violence, extremism, intolerance, and mistrust.

For a while, I had been hearing about the "watching" going on in neighborhoods, college classrooms, and student groups. Then, in 2014, a series of articles by Associated Press reporters Matt Apuzzo and Adam Goldman revealed a special unit of the New York Police Department that targeted Muslim communities in New York City and New Jersey, using many of the techniques depicted in the novel: informants, cameras, and the infiltration of mosques and student organizations. The demographic unit has since been dismantled, though surveillance and sting operations are regular features of counterterrorism operations by law enforcement agencies and the FBI. Recently, after a lawsuit brought by Muslim individuals, mosques, and a nonprofit, arguing that blanket surveillance of Muslim communities was unconstitutional, New York City agreed to appoint an independent civilian to monitor the NYPD's counterterrorism activities.

To learn about surveillance and counterterrorism, please visit marinabudhos.com/books/watched, where I list many of the books, films, websites, and organizations that were vital to the creation of this novel. I consulted many resources to build this story, but all errors are mine.

Watched is not meant to be a conclusive answer, but the opening of a conversation. Please join.

ACKNOWLEDGMENTS

I was born in Jackson Heights, and it is fitting that I finally set one of my novels there. However, this book could not have been written without the help of many generous people who helped me find the story and the way back to the neighborhood of here and now:

Megha Bhouraskar and Minu Tharoor's dinner conversations set me on this path; S. Mitra Kalita served as my guide to Jackson Heights. My friendship and conversations with Annetta Seecharran, former director of SAYA!, and Kavitha Rajagopalan, thinker extraordinaire, were invaluable. Seema Ahmed and Rasel Rahman of Chhaya offered insight into the community and their own personal stories. *New York Times* reporter Matt Apuzzo answered questions on surveillance and informants. Diala Shamas and Ramzi Kassem of CLEAR gave their time and expertise; Ramzi read the manuscript, offering factual corrections. Luis Francia and Midori Yamamura gave me a place to crash, and Neilesh Bose made sure I did not butcher the Bangla. Thanks too to the young people at henna tables on Seventy-Fourth Street who laughed and talked with me.

My dear group—Bonnie, Christina, Alice, Anne, Alex—have buoyed me through the years, along with my Montclair writers' group pals.

The idea of *Watched* was tested with student audiences—thank you, readers, for crowd-sourcing my next book!

William Paterson University granted me Assigned Release Time, while the Virginia Center for the Arts and a grant from the New Jersey State Arts Council gave me refuge for writing. Thanks to John Rowell and John Pietrowski of New Jersey for crucial readings.

Thank you to Stacey Barney for your support over the years, and to Sue Bartle, for nagging me to get on with "your" book.

Early chapters were sensitively read by Sangeeta Mehta, Shirley Budhos, and Deborah Wolfe. Sasha Aronson—now you have to read the whole thing! Rafi Aronson—you're not far behind.

Marc Aronson—as always—present for every step and worry, every hopeful hour.

Wendy Lamb and Dana Carey: I have felt in secure, thoughtful, and inspiring hands. You know how to respect the process while pushing me further than I thought possible. Thank you to Colleen Fellingham and Alison Kolani for meticulous, patient copyediting. I'm grateful to Angela Carlino for her striking cover design, and for her attention to each stage, and to Ken Crossland for the interior.